Samuel French Acting Edition

Southern Comfort

Book & Lyrics by
Dan Collins

D1636313

Music by
Julianne Wick Davis

Based on the Film by
Kate Davis

Conceived for the Stage by
Robert DuSold & Thomas Caruso

SAMUELFRENCH.COM   SAMUELFRENCH.CO.UK

FOR PRODUCTION ENQUIRIES

UNITED STATES AND CANADA
Info@SamuelFrench.com
1-866-598-8449

UNITED KINGDOM AND EUROPE
Plays@SamuelFrench.co.uk
020-7255-4302

Each title is subject to availability from Samuel French, depending
upon country of performance. Please be aware that SOUTHERN
COMFORT may not be licensed by Samuel French in your territory.
Professional and amateur producers should contact the nearest Samuel
French office or licensing partner to verify availability.

MUSIC USE NOTE

Licensees are solely responsible for obtaining formal written permission from copyright owners to use copyrighted music in the performance of this play and are strongly cautioned to do so. If no such permission is obtained by the licensee, then the licensee must use only original music that the licensee owns and controls. Licensees are solely responsible and liable for all music clearances and shall indemnify the copyright owners of the play(s) and their licensing agent, Samuel French, against any costs, expenses, losses and liabilities arising from the use of music by licensees. Please contact the appropriate music licensing authority in your territory for the rights to any incidental music.

IMPORTANT BILLING AND CREDIT REQUIREMENTS

If you have obtained performance rights to this title, please refer to your licensing agreement for important billing and credit requirements.

SOUTHERN COMFORT was first presented as an Actors Equity Showcase at the CAP21 Theatre Company in New York, New York and opened on October 6, 2011. The showcase was directed by Thomas Caruso, with sets by James J. Fenton, costumes by Patricia E. Doherty, lighting by Ed McCarthy, and musical direction by Emily Otto. The Production Stage Manager was Joan Cappello. The cast was as follows:

ROBERT .... Anette O'Toole
LOLA .... Jeff McCarthy
JACKSON... Jeffrey Kuhn
CARLY.. Natalie Joy Johnson
SAM.. Todd Cerveris
MELANIE .... Robin Skye
STORYTELLERS .... Allison Briner, Lizzie Hagstedt,
David Lutken, Joel Waggoner

SOUTHERN COMFORT received its World Premiere production at Barrington Stage Company (Julianne Boyd, Artistic Director; William Finn, Artistic Producer, Musical Theatre Lab) in Pittsfield, Massachusetts and opened on July 24, 2013. The production was directed by Thomas Caruso, with sets by James J. Fenton, costumes by Patricia E. Doherty, lighting by Ed McCarthy, and musical direction by Emily Otto. The Production Stage Manager was Joan Cappello. The cast was as follows:

ROBERT .... Anette O'Toole
LOLA .... Jeff McCarthy
JACKSON... Jeffrey Kuhn
CARLY.. Natalie Joy Johnson
SAM.. Todd Cerveris
MELANIE .... Robin Skye
STORYTELLERS .... Lizzie Hagstedt, Elizabeth Ward Land,
David Lutken, Joel Waggoner

SOUTHERN COMFORT received its New York City Premiere production at The Public Theater (Oskar Eustis, Artistic Director; Patrick Willingham, Executive Director) in New York, New York and opened on March 8, 2016. The production was directed by Thomas Caruso, with sets by James J. Fenton, costumes by Patricia E. Doherty, lighting by Ed McCarthy, and musical direction by David Lutken. The Production Stage Manager was Buzz Cohen. The cast was as follows:

ROBERT .... Anette O'Toole
LOLA .... Jeff McCarthy
JACKSON... Jeffrey Kuhn

CARLY . . . . Aneesh Sheth

SAM . . . . Donnie Cianciotto

MELANIE . . . . Robin Skye

STORYTELLERS . . . . Lizzie Hagstedt, Elizabeth Ward Land,
David Lutken, Joel Waggoner,
Morgan Morse

SOUTHERN COMFORT received a developmental reading at Playwrights Horizons in February 2011.

SOUTHERN COMFORT was supported in part by the National Fund for New Musicals, a program of the National Alliance for Musical Theatre, which also previously supported this show's reading at Playwrights Horizons (2011) and developmental production at CAP21 (2011). Southern Comfort was presented at the National Alliance for Musical Theatre's Festival of New Musicals in 2012 (www.namt.org).

CHARACTERS

ROBERT – Transgender man: A wiry, "electric" man in his fifties. He has the ability to seem like a wide-eyed child and a wise old prophet all at once.

LOLA – Transgender woman: A tall, broad-shouldered woman; somewhat uncomfortable in her own skin. Professionally she still assumes the identity of John. Mid-forties.

JACKSON – Transgender man: A little elf of a man; full of warmth and mischief but struggling with a deep resentment and anger at the world around him. Late thirties/early forties.

CARLY – Transgender woman: Jackson's girlfriend. A naughty Catholic school boy turned naughty Catholic school girl; tough, feminine, and confident. Late twenties/early thirties.

SAM – Transgender man: A hefty, introverted man. He might almost be intimidating, were it not for his extremely gentle and somewhat sad demeanor. Late thirties/early forties.

MELANIE – Cisgender woman: Sam's wife. Spirited and full of good humor, but apprehensive of the world around her. Early/mid-forties.

STORYTELLERS – An onstage folk band that serves as the "orchestra" and storytellers for the show; acting as all the characters in the piece aside from the primary six. They are the passing time and the changing seasons, Robert's parents, the haunting voices of his doctors, and so on. They serve as the storytelling backbone to our "Modern-Day Folk Tale," while also embodying the environment/atmosphere/world around our primary characters – both physically and musically.

For the purposes of identification in the script, the individual members of the **STORYTELLERS** are referred to as: **ELIZABETH, DAVID, JOEL, LIZZIE,** and **MORGAN,** who play percussion, guitar, violin, and bass respectively (the pianist does not sing or perform any roles).

SETTING

Toccoa and Atlanta, Georgia.

TIME

Spring – Winter 1998.

SCENES AND SONGS

ACT ONE

Scene One: The Tree / Spring

Scene Two: Robert's Yard / Barbecue

Scene Three: Robert's Yard / Sunset

Scene Four: Lola's Car / Robert's House / Sunset (Cont.)

Scene Five: Lola's House

Scene Five (A): Summer / Transition to Scene Six

Scene Six: Jackson's House

Scene Seven: Sam & Melanie's House

Scene Eight: Jackson's House / Sam's Journey

Scene Nine: Robert's House / Jackson's House/ Sam & Melanie's House

ACT TWO

Scene One: Fall / Transition to Scene Two

Scene Two: The Southern Comfort Conference (SoCo) - Lobby

Scene Three: SoCo - The Passing Seminar

Scene Four: The Flower Shop / Lola's Room

ACT ONE

Scene One: The Tree / Spring

(We enter the space as though entering Robert's backyard. This is the touchstone throughout the show and the most literal and grounded location – the rest of the scenes grow out of the backyard like conjured memories from a gathering of good friends. The foliage is neutral at this point; somewhat stagnant and bare. Lights reveal **JACKSON, CARLY, MELANIE,** *and* **SAM** *standing in a semi-circle around a small evergreen tree in the yard. The* **STORYTELLERS** *[***ELIZABETH, JOEL, LIZZIE,** *and* **DAVID***] are situated onstage as well, visible to the audience. They do not occupy a "separate space," but instead are always aware of – sometimes even responsive to and/ or affected by – the action around them.)*

[MUSIC NO. 01 "SPRING"]

ELIZABETH.

UNDERNEATH A FROZEN GEORGIA HILL

STORYTELLERS.

UNDER A WICKED CHILL THAT'S
GOT YOU FROZEN STILL

JOEL.

SOMEWHERE, SOMEPLACE UNDERNEATH THAT GROUND

STORYTELLERS.

THERE'S LIVIN' ALL AROUND

READY FOR BEIN' FOUND
READY FOR BEIN' FOUND

LIZZIE.

OVER HEAVY CLOUDS ALL GATHERED TIGHT

STORYTELLERS.

OVER AN ENDLESS NIGHT
THAT STRANGLES OUT THE LIGHT

DAVID.

SOMEWHERE, SOMEPLACE UP ABOVE THE GREY

STORYTELLERS.

THERE IS A BRAND NEW DAY
READY TO SHINE AWAY
READY TO SHINE AWAY

DOWN WITH HOLLOW EMPTY SKIES OF GREY
DOWN WITH FROZEN OVER FLAT DECAY
UP WITH YELLOW, UP WITH GREEN
UP WITH EV'RY COLOR IN BETWEEN
DOWN WITH EARLY DARKNESS AND DESPAIR
UP WITH SPRING
OH SPRING UP EV'RYWHERE

JACKSON. Ain't it always the way? The ones who are so full up on livin' that you could drown in 'em are the ones that life turns around to hit back the hardest.

CARLY. Cuz it knows it's the only hope it's got to knock 'em down.

SAM. That's gotta be the case with Robert Eads...

MELANIE. Lord, he had some kind o' fight in him.

> *(Throughout the following, the characters set flowers, etc. around the stage, slowly and subtly transforming the foliage in the yard into a vibrant spring palate.)*

ELIZABETH.

IN THE VACANT BRANCHES HANGING BARE

STORYTELLERS.

INSIDE THE NAKED THERE
OUT IN THE OPEN AIR

LIZZIE.
SOMEWHERE, SOMEPLACE DEEP INSIDE IS NEW

STORYTELLERS.
AND NOW ITS TIME IS DUE
READY FOR BREAKIN' THROUGH
READY FOR BREAKIN' THROUGH

SAM. His "Chosen Family." That's what he called us.

JACKSON. Most would o' just called us a freak show but... we were family. Not by blood; just by circumstances... "good fortune" as Robert puts it.

MELANIE. We'd see each other one Sunday every month. Without fail.

SAM. And holidays were no exception... Remember Easter?

JACKSON. Resurrection Day.

STORYTELLERS.
DOWN WITH EMPTY BARREN SLEEPING TREES
DOWN WITH CUTTING COLD THAT STINGS THE BREEZE
UP WITH LAVENDER, UP WITH BLUE
UP WITH LIVING REALLY COMING TRUE
DOWN WITH HOPELESSNESS THAT STRIPS YOU BARE
UP WITH SPRING
OH SPRING UP EVERYWHERE

MORGAN.	**STORYTELLERS.**
SOMETHING REAL UNDERNEATH THE COLD	AH

STORYTELLERS.
READY READY TO BREAK GROUND

JOEL.	**STORYTELLERS.**
SOMETHING TRUE AND TRYIN' TO TAKE HOLD	AH

STORYTELLERS.
READY READY TO BE FOUND

ELIZABETH.	**STORYTELLERS.**
SOMETHING CAN'T WAIT ANYMORE TO START	AH

STORYTELLERS.
READY READY TO TAKE SHAPE

JOEL.   **STORYTELLERS.**

SOMETHING AT THE WALLS INSIDE YOUR   AH
HEART

STORYTELLERS.

READY READY TO ESCAPE

LIZZIE.   **STORYTELLERS.**

SOMETHING SOMEBODY ONCE SAID TO   AH
YOU

STORYTELLERS.

HAUNTS YOU LIKE A BITTER STING

ELIZABETH.   **STORYTELLERS.**

SOMETHING IN YOU KNOWS IT ISN'T   AH
TRUE

STORYTELLERS.

LET IT UP AND LET IT SPRING... AH

(The yard is vibrant and alive now.)

JACKSON.

DOWN WITH ONE MORE DARK AND DISMAL DAY

CARLY.

DOWN WITH DWELLING ON THE COLD DECAY

MELANIE.

UP WITH CHERRY BLOSSOMS UP WITH RED

SAM.

UP WITH FAR AWAY FROM BEIN' DEAD

CARLY.

DOWN WITH LAYING UNDERNEATH THE CHILL

MELANIE.

DOWN WITH FREEZING UP AND STANDING STILL

JACKSON.

UP WITH TURNING YOURSELF TO THE SUN
UP WITH MOVIN' CUZ THE PAST IS DONE

ALL (EXCEPT ROBERT & LOLA).

DOWN WITH LIVING YOUR LIFE UNDER THERE
UP WITH SPRING
OH SPRING UP
UP WITH SPRING

OH SPRING UP
UP WITH SPRING
OH SPRING UP
UP WITH SPRING
OH SPRING UP EVERYWHERE...

(Lights fade...)

EVERYWHERE
EVERYWHERE...

Scene Two: Robert's Yard / Barbecue

*(**ROBERT** is isolated in a spot of light, looking out over the audience as if addressing them:)*

ROBERT. Toccoa, Georgia. This here is bubba land. Home o' the bubba. The good ole boys. Oh yes. I met this fella at Walmart. I was sittin' outside havin' my pipe; he was out smokin' his. And we got to chattin'. And he starts tellin' me 'bout this group he belongs to. He just knew I'd fit right in with the organization. Turns out it's a shoot off o' the KKK –

*(Lights rise fully to reveal **SAM** and **MELANIE** preparing a picnic table for lunch.)*

MELANIE.	SAM.
Robert!	You kiddin'?

ROBERT. N' they're askin' *me* to join their group. I love it.

MELANIE. You love the KKK?

ROBERT.	SAM.
No. No. No.	That ain't what he means.

ROBERT. It just goes to show: you give people half a chance... they accept you without realizin'.

SAM. So...you joinin'?

MELANIE. You are not!

*(**SAM** laughs. He is trying to get **MELANIE** worked up.)*

ROBERT. I can just imagine if I walked into their meetin'; introduced myself and tell 'em what I am. I imagine it'd be...quite a scene.

(Noticing something offstage.)

What's that?

MELANIE. *(Momentarily frightened.)* What? *Where?*

ROBERT. *(Speaking to someone offstage.)* I think... Yep. It's an honest to goodness leprechaun!

*(**JACKSON** enters.)*

JACKSON. *(To* **ROBERT.***)* You would know.

ROBERT. How's that?

JACKSON. Well, let's see – it's 1998. And you were born in 19...million B.C. So yeah, you were right there when they started up mythology.

ROBERT. C'mere ingrate.

(**JACKSON** *and* **ROBERT** *hug and kiss. Then* **JACKSON** *moves to* **SAM** *and* **MELANIE:***)*

MELANIE.	**SAM.**	**JACKSON.**
Happy Sunday.	Hey dude. Happy Sunday.	Hey, Sam. Melanie. Happy Sunday.

JACKSON. Am I the rotten Easter egg?

SAM. No, we're waitin' on Lola still.

JACKSON. *(To* **ROBERT.***)* Lord, next to half a year we been waitin' to meet this mystery girl o' yours, and now she's gonna keep us waitin' even longer?

MELANIE. Oh hush. I know she'll be worth the wait.

ROBERT. Guarantee it, I was waitin' my whole life and she's still worth it.

JACKSON. *(Rolling his eyes.)* Oh brother.

ROBERT. *(To* **SAM**, *in reference to* **JACKSON***; playfully.)* This comin' from the guy who's got a new girl every month.

JACKSON. Yeah, but I never make you meet any o' them!

(**JACKSON** *laughs and elbows* **SAM**, *who laughs with him. Then, surveying the table:)*

So where's your girl sittin', Pops?

ROBERT. Right next to me there.

JACKSON. Nah, that's my chair.

ROBERT. Why's that?

JACKSON. Cuz I'm your son.

SAM. You do remember he didn't actually bring you into this world; right, Jack?

ROBERT. Watch it, wise guy; y'all are like family to me. But Jackson... I saw him through from Peggy Sue to who he is now; that's as much bringing life into this world as anyone, far as I'm concerned.

But you're still sittin' over there.

(JACKSON sets up the extra chair at the table.)

MELANIE. *(Hearing something offstage.)* Is that her?

(A moment.)

Nevermind. I guess I'm kind o' nervous. It's always been just us on these Sundays, feels weird. I mean, exciting, but...

ROBERT. Well I appreciate all you bein' here to meet her.

(Raising his beer bottle.)

Happy Easter.

(Everyone clinks glasses.)

I know none of us really got the choice to be with our families today – our biological ones. But that don't mean we got no choice at all. And bein' here with all you, well – I wouldn't have it any other way.

JACKSON. The Prophet o' Toccoa strikes again.

(SAM and MELANIE laugh as everyone drinks in response to the toast. ROBERT falters slightly in his step as he maneuvers around the grill – Brief, tense glances pass between SAM, MEL, and JACKSON.)

Hey, why not take a seat n' gimme a turn at that grill?

ROBERT. Because I want the food to have flavor.

(Laughter from SAM and MELANIE.)

C'mon, lighten up Leprechaun. It's Easter. *Resurrection* Day...

(JACKSON is about to respond –)

[MUSIC NO. 02 "CHOSEN FAMILY"]

ROBERT.

NOT ANOTHER WORD
NOT A WHISPER 'BOUT A SICKNESS
OR A QUIVER ON THE LIPS THAT MIGHT BECOME A
FROWN
JUST ENJOY THE DAY
GO ON SIMPLY BE A WITNESS
TO THE BLESSINGS GIVEN US FROM ALL AROUND

THERE'S CHARCOAL ON THE AIR

SAM.

AND THE SMELL IS NEXT TO HEAVEN

MELANIE.

THERE'S SHININ' SUN AND BREEZES MOVIN' OVER ME

SAM.

COOKIN'S ALMOST DONE

JACKSON.

N' MY APPETITE IS REVVIN'

ALL FOUR.

AND THERE'S NO PLACE IN THE WORLD I WOULD RATHER
BE

ROBERT.

SOMEWHERE SUNLIGHT MIGHT BE WARMER
BUT NOTHIN'S BRIGHTER THAN YOUR COMPANY
SOME SAY THIS MIGHT NOT BE NORMAL
BUT HOME IS RIGHT HERE WITH MY CHOSEN FAMILY

SO NOT A SINGLE WORD
'BOUT THE FOLK WHO WENT AND LEFT US

JACKSON.

AIN'T NO WORRIES THERE

JACKSON & SAM.

CUZ WE AIN'T GOT THE TIME

ROBERT.

DOESN'T MATTER, THOUGH

SAM. *(Hugging* **MELANIE.***)*
>CUZ THE FOLK WHO WENT AND KEPT US

ALL FOUR.
>MAKE ME THANKFUL EV'RY DAY THIS LIFE IS MINE

ALL FOUR & STORYTELLERS.
>SOMEWHERE BREEZES MIGHT BE SWEETER

ROBERT.
>BUT NO SUGAR WIND CAN BEAT YOUR COMPANY

ALL FOUR & STORYTELLERS.
>SOME SAY BLOOD IS THICKER THAN WATER

ROBERT.
>BUT THEY AIN'T NEVER MET MY CHOSEN FAMILY

>FAMILY'S AN ICEBERG WE RIDE INTO THE SEA

MELANIE. Here we go.

ROBERT.
>THE PARTS THAT BREAK AWAY WE GOTTA LOSE
>BUT IT COULD MELT ENTIRELY AND I KNOW I'D STILL BE
>KEPT ABOVE THE WATER BY THE FAMILY I CHOOSE

>*(Everyone rushes to finalize setting the table/ food for lunch.)*

MELANIE.	JACKSON.	ROBERT.
NOT ANOTHER WORD		
NOT UNTIL THIS TABLE'S		SOMEWHERE
READY	THERE I SET THE	SUNLIGHT MIGHT
	MUSTARD!	BE WARMER
SAM.		BUT NOTHING'S
DID ANYONE BRING BAKED		BRIGHTER THAN
BEANS?	*(To* **SAM,** *referring to* **MELANIE***:)*	YOUR COMPANY
	ISN'T THIS HER JOB?	

MELANIE.

(*To* **JACKSON.**)
YOU BETTER
WATCH THAT
MOUTH

JACKSON & MELANIE.
(*Referring to the
beer.*)

PASS ONE HERE
TO ME

MELANIE.
(*Opening a
container...*)
DID ANYBODY
SMELL THIS?

ROBERT.

SOMEWHERE
TABLES MIGHT
BE
FULLER
BUT NOTHIN'
FILLS
ME UP

SAM.
(*Looking in the
cooler.*)
WHO ELSE
WANTS A
BEER?

NOTHIN' FILLS
ME
UP

LORD I'M NEXT
TO
STARVIN'

NO, NOTHIN'
FILLS ME
UP

JACKSON.
(*To* **ROBERT.**)
WHERE THE
HECK IS
YOUR
GIRLFRIEND?

LIKE MY
CHOSEN
FAMILY

(*As the song ends, a spot illuminates* **LOLA***;
a tall, statuesque woman standing on the
opposite side of the stage. It isn't just the
fact that the rest are grouped together on
the opposite end of the stage that makes
her seem a million miles away from them.
The others –* **MELANIE** *included – are dressed
casually; flannels, sweatshirts, jeans, etc.*
LOLA*, in contrast, wears a loudly-colored*

polyester pant suit, an all-too-perfectly-bobbed wig, and large sunglasses. In spite of the boldness that her outfit might suggest, her awkwardness in her own skin is palpable; as though she wishes she could collapse into herself. She carries a store-bought container of hummus.)

ROBERT. *(Noticing* **LOLA***.)* Well ain't you a sight.

LOLA. Sorry...the traffic –

ROBERT. No sorrys, you're here now; all that matters.

*(***ROBERT*** *pulls* **LOLA** *into the group.)*

Lola: Melanie, Sam, and Jackson.

Melanie, Sam, and Jackson: Miss Lola Cola!

(An awkward silence...as though the others are in slight shock...)

JACKSON. C'mon Pops, you gotta acclimate her a little more than that or she's likely to get a headache wonderin' what's what.

(He approaches **LOLA** *and shakes her hand.)*

I'm Jackson, born Peggy Sue. N' don't let Sam there fool you –

MELANIE. *Jack!*

JACKSON. Now Mel, believe it or not, was born an actual, biological woman.

ROBERT. And Jack – *"believe it or not"* – has absolutely no manners or sense o' decency –

JACKSON. Hey, just havin' some fun – ain't we allowed to be a little indecent 'round family?

LOLA. Well. This all looks so nice. I brought some sundried tomato hummus.

(Glances suggest that this might be the most disgusting thing anyone has ever heard.)

ROBERT. *(Takes it from her and gives her a kiss.)* She's very worldly...

(Bringing the hummus to the table and setting it smack in the middle.)

...lives practically in Atlanta, right?

MELANIE. Well, we'll have to get you a little closer to us in Toccoa. We do this every month, the gas money alone'll do you in!

LOLA. Oh, well... I already stick out like a sore thumb where I'm at. I could only imagine...way out here.

ROBERT. Well what're we waitin' for. Sit down, sit down.

*(**ROBERT** guides **LOLA** to "Jackson's chair." **JACKSON** begrudgingly sits on the other side of **ROBERT**. Everyone is seated...)*

This is all I could ask for, right here...

[MUSIC NO. 03 "GRACE"]

SOMEWHERE SUNLIGHT MIGHT BE WARMER
BUT NOTHIN'S BRIGHTER THAN YOUR COMPANY
SOME SAY THIS MIGHT NOT BE NORMAL
BUT HOME IS RIGHT HERE WITH MY CHOSEN FAMILY

*(The music continues/softens as **MELANIE** leans into **SAM**'s arms, **LOLA** leans into **ROBERT**'s, and **JACKSON** stands center. They seem almost frozen in a tableau. The lights dim and shift us into...)*

Scene Three: Robert's Yard / Sunset

(**ROBERT**, **LOLA**, **SAM**, **MELANIE**, *and* **JACKSON** *remain in their tableau as the lights suggest the passage of time and the sunset.* **LOLA** *stares at nothing; deep in thought.*)

ROBERT. Hey.

(**LOLA** *snaps out of her daze.*)

You okay?

LOLA. Fine, I... I just shouldn't have worn this. I thought it'd be nice but...

ROBERT. You look beautiful.

LOLA. I look ridiculous.

ROBERT. You look like a dream.

LOLA. Stop.

ROBERT. (*Playfully whispering into her ear as she leans into his arms.*) A wet dream.

LOLA. *Robert.*

(*Craning her neck to look him in the face.*)

You're so...

ROBERT. What?

LOLA. Cute.

ROBERT. Cute? I ain't a stuffed toy. How 'bout handsome?

(*He tickles her. She giggles and tries to squirm away.*)

How 'bout rugged?

(*He tickles her again.*)

How 'bout the burly man o' your dreams?

(*She still squirms to escape.*)

Okay, I'm done. I'm sorry. Here. Lay back.

(*She settles back into his arms.*)

But don't call me cute again.

(She smiles and sinks further into his arms.)

JACKSON. Lord, no one warned me this was gonna be a girly party.

MELANIE. *What?*

JACKSON. All this lovey dovey under the stars.

ROBERT. He's just jealous.

> *(The **STORYTELLERS** seem to pick up on the playful energy around them – expressing themselves with a musical gesture that hints at the song to come:)*

[MUSIC NO. 04 "WOMEN"]

JACKSON. Jealous? No sir, I don't need any o' that nonsense.

MELANIE. What nonsense?

> *(Another musical gesture, "egging them on.")*

JACKSON. You know, *womenly* nonsense.

> *(The musical gestures begin to solidify into the song...)*

MELANIE. Are you kiddin'?

JACKSON. Mm-mm *(I.e. "nope.")*. The grass on that side o' the fence is a foreign world to me.

> *(Laughter from **SAM** and **ROBERT**.)*

JACKSON.
THEY'LL MAKE SENSE
　　FROM A WHOLE LOTTA
　　NONSENSE
THEN MAKE NONSENSE
　　RIGHT OUT OF A FACT　**MELANIE.**
YOU CAN TURN BLUE　　　　Lola, I think we gotta stick
　　TRY'N' TO FIGHT 'EM　　up for ourselves!
BUT THERE AIN'T NO
　　SENSE DOIN' THAT
LOLA.
　　Oh, well...

JACKSON.

> CUZ OIL DON'T MIX UP WITH WATER
> THE MOON DON'T COME UP WITH THE SUN
> OH WOMEN, LORD THEY
> WERE NEVER THIS WAY
> BACK WHEN I USED TO BE ONE

MELANIE. *Jackson!* Talk about nonsense…

JACKSON. C'mon Sam, ain't it true?

SAM. Uh –

MELANIE. "Uh"? What do you got to "Uh" about?

JACKSON. *(Coming around* **SAM** *and tickling him.)* C'mon. Tell her.

SAM. Well…

MELANIE. Don't you dare, mister.

SAM.

(Flirtatiously, chasing **MELANIE**, *hugging her, etc.)*

MELANIE.

> SOMETIMES THEY BEG YOU TO BUILD 'EM A BIRD HOUSE

You loved doin' that!

> AND THEN NAG ABOUT THE BIRDS IN THE YARD

…One time, and it wasn't even –

> THEN THE BIRDS N' THE BEES IS ALL THEY REALLY WANT
> THEN THE NEXT NIGHT THEY WANNA COUNT STARS

…Sam!

> CHASIN' YA DOWN 'TIL YOU WANT 'EM

…You won't be catchin' *me* any time soon mister!

> THEN GOIN' RIGHT BACK ON THE RUN RUN RUN
> OH WOMEN, LORD THEY
> WERE NEVER THIS WAY

BACK WHEN I USED TO BE ONE

JACKSON.

BACK BEFORE I EVER STARTED SHAVIN' MY FACE

MELANIE.

AND BEFORE YOU STARTED SHAVIN' YOUR BACK

(**ROBERT** *busts out laughing.*)

JACKSON. *(To the amused* **MELANIE.***)*

BACK BEFORE MELANIE WENT AND FOUND HUSBAND SIX

JACKSON & SAM.

AND BEFORE HER UPPER LIP NEEDED WAX

MELANIE. *Stop it!*

JACKSON & SAM.

BEFORE I KNEW YOU

AND BEFORE YA KNEW ME

BEFORE WE FOUND THE WAY BACK TO OUR FAMILY TREE

BEFORE YOU KNEW YOU

AND BEFORE I KNEW ME

N' BEFORE OUR MUSCLES GOT SO BIG IT'S ALL YOU

COULD SEE

ROBERT. C'mon now, y'all know gender's got nothin' more to do with that kind o' stuff than it has to do with what's between your legs. The truth is inside.

SAM. And the scars are outside.

MELANIE. Sam –

SAM. I'm just sayin': after how them doctors messed up my chest, I sure ain't gonna let 'em do nothin' down there. 'Specially not no phalloplasty –

LOLA. No *what*?

(*A shocked silence. Music comes to a screeching halt.*)

JACKSON. You don't know what a phalloplasty is?

LOLA. Oh…sorry. Is that the word for the um…artificial…

(*She motions at her lap, then stops herself – awkwardly:*)

I mean –

MELANIE. Good Lord. Can't we just talk about bunnies or Easter eggs or somethin' common for a change?!

ROBERT. Well I got somethin' to talk about...but it sure ain't common...

>   *(He takes **LOLA** by the hand.)*

JACKSON. Oh brother...

ROBERT.

> WELL SHE MIGHT AS
>   WELL A' BEEN ON A
>   MOUNTAIN
> CUZ SHE WAS SO FAR OUT
>   A' MY REACH
> BUT NOW I'M ALL DIZZY N'
>   GIDDY
> FROM THE AIR UP WHERE
>   WE'RE SHARIN' THE
>   PEAK
> WELL I'VE SEEN SOME
>   BEAUTY IN MY TIME
> BUT NOW ALL MY LOOKIN'
>   IS DONE
> WOMEN, LORD THEY
> WERE NEVER THIS WAY
> BACK WHEN I USED TO BE ONE

LOLA.

> *(Blushing.)* Stop, red is not my color!

JACKSON.

> 'Course he'd make it all romantic –

MELANIE.

> Hush!

ROBERT, JACKSON & SAM.

> OH WOMEN LORD THEY
> WERE NEVER THIS WAY
> BACK WHEN I USED TO
> BACK WHEN I
> BACK WHEN I USED TO BE ONE

>   *(**ROBERT** is close – dancing with and flirtatiously pecking **LOLA** as the song ends.)*

JACKSON. Lord almighty. Snap out of it Pops, this ain't SoCo.

>   *(Laughter from **SAM** and **MELANIE**.)*

LOLA. Ain't what?

JACKSON. *(To* **ROBERT.***)* You ain't even told her about SoCo?

ROBERT. *(To* **LOLA.***)* He means Southern Comfort.

LOLA. Oh. That's the big conference in Atlanta, for...um –

JACKSON. Freaks like us.

ROBERT. Speak for yourself.

LOLA. You call it SoCo?

JACKSON. Everyone does.

ROBERT. She ain't never been.

MELANIE. Oh Lola, you gotta!

SAM. We take over the whole Sheraton Hotel. Couple others too; they love us!

MELANIE. Oh, the Southern Comfort Conference is... You just gotta! It's like a big ol' family reunion, but a good one. And then o' course: on the last day, there's The Ball. Bein' able to dance and hold each other like that without worryin' 'bout...who's around. It's like prom all over.

ROBERT. Which reminds me, I gotta check how my tux fits. Where'd we box that thing up after last year, Jack?

JACKSON. Ain't no sense doin' it now. I mean... SoCo's a ways off, and with the way you been losin' weight –

MELANIE.	**SAM.**
Hush.	Jack.

    (Tense looks pass between the group.)

ROBERT. Okay, while y'all are bein' awkward, I'm gonna go take a look at those stars poppin' out.

    *(***JACKSON** *and* **LOLA** *move to follow.)*

...by *myself.* Y'all visit some.

    *(***ROBERT** *moves away;* **JACKSON***,* **LOLA***,* **SAM***, and* **MELANIE** *stand awkwardly side by side. A long moment, then:)*

LOLA. *(To* **JACKSON.***)* I love these colors on your flannel, they're so...you know, warm. Which is perfect for flannel, you know?

JACKSON. Thanks. Um...that's a nice blouse; helps cut the shoulders down.

MELANIE. Jack.

JACKSON. No. I didn't mean that in a... I mean, I know that's something that a lot o' girls like you struggle with and...I...

(*Awkward beat.*)

You wanna beer? Er...a wine cooler...?

LOLA. No no, I'm... I actually should be going.

ROBERT. (*Overhearing her.*) Goin'?

LOLA. It's late and...I've got that ride ahead of me.

MELANIE. Yeah, we probably oughta get on our way too, right?

(*To* **LOLA.**)

C'mon sweetie, we'll walk you out.

Robert, a pleasure as always.

ROBERT.	SAM.	JACKSON.	MELANIE.	LOLA.
All mine.	Thanks, man.	Take it easy y'all.	(*To* **JACK.**)	Goodnight.
	You too.		You behave yourself.	Thank you.
Same time next month.	Ain't Jackson hosting?	Yes ma'am.		
Don't remind him!	(*To* **MEL.**)	Month after next.		
	We got everything else?	Ha. Ha.		
Yep!	Okay, y'all!		Bye, loves!	

(**LOLA** *hurries to exit with* **SAM** *and* **MELANIE** – **ROBERT** *intercepts her.*)

ROBERT. Hold on now, where's my goodbye?

LOLA. Oh, sorry...

> (**JACKSON** *sits at the table, still in their vicinity.* **LOLA** *gives* **ROBERT** *a quick/awkward peck and whispers "Bye," with a sidelong glance at* **JACKSON**, *before quickly exiting.*)

Thank you.

ROBERT. Bye!

So?

JACKSON. So.

ROBERT. *(Preparing his pipe.)* What did you think?

JACKSON. ...'Bout?

ROBERT. *(Laughing.)* Lola.

JACKSON. *(Picking up the untouched hummus from the table.)* She's worldly.

ROBERT. Worldly?

JACKSON. *(Changing the subject.)* You gonna share that tobacco?

ROBERT. *(Handing the tobacco to* **JACKSON**.*)* I should o' started keepin' a tab for you, could o' bought myself a couple o' acres by now.

JACKSON. Who needs acres – you got the finest square inch in Toccoa.

ROBERT. Hey now, don't knock it. Ain't nothin' better in this world than land. It's home while you're livin' on it and it's what you leave behind when you're gone.

JACKSON. Shoot, you tellin' me this is all gonna be mine one day?

ROBERT. Says who?

JACKSON. You think I been lettin' you call me son all these years for nothin'?

ROBERT. Well this is real touchin'.

JACKSON. So do I get that Charlie Brown Christmas tree too?

ROBERT. Ain't no Charlie Brown tree. That there was a foot high when I first moved in. Another ten years, they'll be askin' to haul it off to Rockefeller.

JACKSON. Rockefeller? For Christ's sake –

ROBERT. Watch your mouth. That's disrespect to your maker.

JACKSON. After what our maker's done to you, don't see that he deserves my respect.

> (*Stark lights illuminate the* **STORYTELLERS** *as they embody the* **DOCTORS**.)

DOCTOR 1. Miss Eads, we've received the results of the biopsy...

> (**ROBERT** *shakes off the voice.*)

JACKSON. Here you are livin' your life more honestly than most folk. N' what's God do?

DOCTOR 2. I'm sorry...ma'am...

ROBERT. (*Holding his head as if battling a headache.*) Please. Don't –

JACKSON. He slaps you with stage four cancer –

ROBERT. Son –

DOCTOR 2. I'm afraid the cancer has metastasized...

JACKSON. And not just any cancer. *No.*

DOCTOR 1. I'm sorry; ma'am.

JACKSON. Your ovaries, Robert, your goddamn –

ROBERT. Hey –

JACKSON. The last and only part o' you that's still female and he's tryin' to kill you with it.

ROBERT. *That's enough.*

> (*A beat.*)

Sorry, but –

JACKSON. Nah, I'm sorry, Pops. I just. I don't know how you ain't angry every second o' every day.

> (*A beat.*)

ROBERT. Worldly.

JACKSON. (*What?*) Hm?

ROBERT. That's all you got to say about Lola?

JACKSON. *(Laughing.)* You said it.

ROBERT. I'm thinkin' o' askin' her to go to Southern Comfort with me.

JACKSON. Really?

ROBERT. What's wrong with that?

JACKSON. Just. I don't get it. How serious you thinkin' o' gettin' with Lola?

ROBERT. *(Playful, but also sort of means it.)* Well, some o' us are lookin' for more than the next bed to jump into.

JACKSON. *(Playing back.)* Lord; here goes the Reverend Eads.

ROBERT. I'm only sayin': Part o' bein' your own man one day is learnin' what a real, intimate relationship is.

JACKSON. Do we not have an intimate relationship?

ROBERT. I'm talkin' about a relationship with a woman. That ain't just sexual. A real commitment might do you good, Jack. I ain't gonna be around forever and –

JACKSON. I know, Pops. That's why I don't want you wastin' any time.

ROBERT. Well it's my time to waste.

JACKSON. No. It's our time too. You know.

(*A beat.*)

Besides; you want'o talk about real commitment; how about Lola's commitment to Lola?

ROBERT. What are you talkin' about?

JACKSON. It's just... *Lola Cola??*

(*Light up on* **LOLA** *as she sits in her car, driving.*)

...Sounds more like a drag queen than a flesh n' blood *person.* I mean, is she even serious 'bout all o' this?

Scene Four: Lola's Car / Robert's House / Sunset (Cont.)

(LOLA sits in a chair representing her car. Suddenly, she looks around herself in concern:)

LOLA. Shoot...

(She tries to keep going.)

C'mon. *Please.*

(No luck. She begins fishing around for something in the glove compartment as the MAN approaches and knocks on the window. Meanwhile...)

JACKSON. I'm just sayin', you sure Southern Comfort is the right place for her? Seems like all she's gotta do is take off that wig and makeup and she's a man.

(Back in LOLA's scene:)

MAN. You alright Miss?

(LOLA is startled and turns to look at him. He motions her to roll down her window... She hesitates. Then complies – keeping her face turned away from him.)

LOLA. Fine I just... I think my tire...

MAN. *(Stepping back and looking at the car.)* Oh yep, sure is.

(Back to ROBERT and JACKSON.)

ROBERT. Now how's what you're sayin' any better than them folk who say we don't count cuz we only got surgery on half of us?

JACKSON. Well, maybe I can see where they're comin' from now.

ROBERT. What're you talkin' about?

JACKSON. I just mean: She's only Lola when it's convenient for her.

(*Meanwhile...*)

MAN. Must be some glass back there on the road – damn kids throwin' beer bottles out the windows – stupid faggots.

LOLA. I can handle it, really –

> (**LOLA** *still has her face turned away from the* **MAN.**)

MAN. Spare's in the trunk I'm sure. Go on gimme them keys.

LOLA. (*Getting out of the car, trying to hunch over to seem less tall.*) I'll get it.

> (*Focus returns to* **ROBERT** *and* **JACKSON.**)

JACKSON. I mean, if she ain't takin' herself seriously; why should I?

ROBERT. You don't even know her.

JACKSON. Neither does she.

> (**ROBERT** *shoots him a challenging look.*)

MAN.	LOLA.	JACKSON.	ROBERT.
You're kind o' tall ain't you?			
	No...		
Kinda...			
	Look, I'm okay,	We just don't need	
You got big heels on or somethin'?	you don't –	that kind o' mess around us	
		right now.	Mess?! What mess?
	What? No, I –	C'mon, Pops. She's doin'	
Don't get testy, I'm just sayin',	I...	that whole bimbo act we hate.	

I don't usually   She ain't
gotta look up at a lady –   doin' no
I...   act. And
                               she ain't a
                               bimbo.

LOLA. *(Puts her hands over her ears and closes her eyes.)*
STOP...

> *(Lights go out on the* **MAN**, **ROBERT**, *and*
> **JACKSON**.*)*

...please.

[MUSIC NO. 05 "BIRD"]

LIZZIE.

> LA LA LA
> LA LA LA
> LA LA LALALA...

LOLA & LIZZIE.

> LA LA LA
> LA LA LA
> LA LA LALALALA...

> *(***LIZZIE** *drops out...)*

LOLA.

> LA LA LA
> LA LA LA
> LA LA LALALALA...

> IS THAT MY VOICE?
> THAT AWFUL GRUMBLING DEEP AND LOW
> WHAT IS THAT SOUND?
> IT BELONGS TO SOMEONE I DON'T KNOW
> BUT WHEN I COME TRUE
> THAT'S WHEN YOU
> SAY I'M PUTTING ON A SHOW

> WHEN I'M ASLEEP
> I SEE MYSELF BEHIND MY EYES
> INSIDE THE DARK
> I'M MORE THAN SOUND AND SHAPE AND SIZE

I'M COMING TRUE
AND WHAT A VIEW
I LOOK OUT AND REALIZE

I'M A BIRD
CAN'T YOU HEAR
HOW I SING SO SWEET AND CLEAR
THAT I NEARLY
NEARLY TOUCH THE SKY
EV'RY WORD
ON A WING
SUCH A PRETTY LITTLE THING
WHEN I SING
WHEN I SING

LOLA & LIZZIE.

LA LA LA
LA LA LA
LA LA LALALA

(**LIZZIE** *drops out…*)

LOLA.

LA LA LA
LA LA LA
LA LA LALALA

SUCH WICKED DREAMS
WAKE ME UP INTO THE CRUEL SOUND
OF MY OWN VOICE
FULL OF GRAVITY IN EV'RY POUND
THIS CAN'T BE TRUE
WHAT CAN I DO
TO GET BACK UP OFF THE GROUND?

GIVE ME THE SKY
FAR AWAY FROM PEOPLE TELLING ME
LOOK AT YOURSELF
THE LORD MADE YOU ONLY WHAT YOU SEE
THAT ISN'T TRUE
I ALWAYS KNEW
THAT HE WANTED ME TO BE

LOLA & LIZZIE.

    LIKE A BIRD
    CAN'T YOU HEAR
    HOW I SING SO SWEET AND CLEAR
    THAT I NEARLY
    NEARLY TOUCH THE SKY
    EV'RY WORD
    ON A WING
    SUCH A PRETTY LITTLE THING
    WHEN I SING
    WHEN I SING
    LA LA LA
    LA LA LA
    LA LA LALALA

LOLA.

    A GENTLE NAME
    A TINY FRAME
    GOODNESS HOW THE BOYS ALL CLING
    AND IN MY DRESS
    NO NEED TO GUESS
    NOBODY'S EVER WONDERING
    NOT A QUESTION
    MY REFLECTION
    ISN'T HIDING ANYTHING
    YOU CAN HEAR IT WHEN I SING
    WHEN I SING

    LIKE A BIRD

LIZZIE.

    I'M A BIRD

LOLA & LIZZIE.

    YOU KNOW ONE DAY I'LL SING SO SWEET AND HIGH

LIZZIE.

    SO SWEET AND HIGH

LOLA & LIZZIE.

    I AM GLIDING IN THE SKY
    EV'RY WORD
    FLOATING BY

SUCH A PRETTY LITTLE THING

LOLA.

LITTLE THING

LIZZIE.

A PRETTY LITTLE THING

LOLA.

A PRETTY LITTLE THING

LOLA & LIZZIE.

YES I'LL BE A PRETTY LITTLE THING

(**LOLA** *removes her wig, blouse, and makeup.*)

LOLA.	**LIZZIE.**
WHEN I FLY	LA LA LA
	LA LA LA
WHEN I FLY	LA LA LALALALA...
	LA LA LALA
WHEN I FLY	LA LA LA
	LA LA LALALALALALA
WHEN I FLY	

LOLA.

FLY

FLY

FLY

FLY...

(*The scene changes to...*)

Scene Five: Lola's House

>(**LOLA** *sits at her computer, stripped of all femininity; she is now* **JOHN**.)

LOLA (JOHN). *(On the phone.)* John's Heating and Cooling... Yes, this is John.

>(*A moment.*)

I told him I don't know until I look at it. Your best case is if it's easily gotten to and just needs to be brushed then, you know, it might be like twenty bucks. But if we have to pull it and recover refrigerant – Look I've got a client with me, can I call you back?

>(*He hangs up. Lights reveal one of the* **STORYTELLERS** *portraying* **MS. MILLER**.)

Sorry.

MS. MILLER. Oh that's fine John. I love to watch a man at work.

LOLA (JOHN). Well thank you Mrs. –

MS. MILLER. *Ms.* Miller.

LOLA (JOHN). Right. So...you're looking to upgrade the duct work in your house to –

>(**ROBERT** *enters with grocery bags in hand.*)

ROBERT. Hello? Your personal Chef has arrived!

LOLA (JOHN). Robert –

ROBERT. Whoops. Still business hours?

LOLA (JOHN). *(Instinctively reaching up to fluff the wig that is not on her head.)* Yes I –

MS. MILLER. Well, well... Who's your friend?

LOLA (JOHN). Oh...

ROBERT. Don't mind me. I'll just be in the kitchen –

LOLA (JOHN). Actually Mrs. Mill–

MS. MILLER. *Ms.*

LOLA (JOHN). If we could continue this conversation tomorrow, I really should –

ROBERT. Don't stop on my account!

LOLA (JOHN). It'll just take me at least twenty-four hours to get you a quote so –

MS. MILLER. You sure you boys don't want a lady's company for dinner?

LOLA (JOHN). Oh, well –

ROBERT. I think we got that taken care of.

MS. MILLER. What?

LOLA (JOHN). He's just... I'll call you tomorrow about –

MS. MILLER. Yes, we gotta get that A.C. workin', cuz it really is gettin'

> (*Subtly flirtatious to* **LOLA (JOHN)**.)

Way too hot.

> (**LOLA (JOHN)** *awkwardly shakes* **MS. MILLER**'s *hand, putting some distance between them.*)

LOLA (JOHN). Okay, well, I'll call you as soon as possible.

MS. MILLER. Tomorrow.

LOLA (JOHN). Tomorrow.

> (**MS. MILLER** *exits.*)

ROBERT. Well, well, well.

LOLA. Robert. What're you doin'? If people here suspected that...

ROBERT. She had no clue... If anything she'll be out there drummin' up business for you. Cuz it really is gettin'... way too hot.

LOLA. Robert! It's not business I'm worried about. You saw that article in the *Augusta Review* last week... One town over that boy was beaten near to death cuz someone saw him out at a gay bar. People like that find out about folk like you and me...we won't be so lucky.

> (**ROBERT** *sits down on the sofa and slaps his knee.*)

ROBERT. C'mere.

LOLA. No.

ROBERT. C'mon.

LOLA. I'll crush you.

ROBERT. You'll only crush me if you stay all the way over there.

> (**LOLA** *smiles in spite of herself and moves over to him and sits on his lap.*)

LOLA. There.

> (**ROBERT** *dips her off his knee so that she falls back onto the couch. She squeals and laughs as he moves in and gives her a kiss.*)

You smell like that pipe.

ROBERT. *(Going in for another kiss.)* Thank you.

LOLA. You really should stop doin' that, you know.

ROBERT. Hey, I'm just tryin' to get some cancer goin' in the lungs too.

LOLA. *Stop.*

> (**ROBERT** *just takes her in for a second; big, silly smile.*)

What?

ROBERT. You're beautiful.

LOLA. I could be wearing a burlap sack and flippers and you'd still say that.

ROBERT. It's true.

LOLA. It's cute.

ROBERT. Now what did I say about that word?

LOLA. *(Laughing – she can't help herself.)* Maybe I'm just gettin' even for you bargin' in on me when I'm not... myself.

ROBERT. Well I'm only bargin' in cuz I gotta ask you somethin' real important.

LOLA. What?

ROBERT. Well. Ms. Lola Cola, I wanted to do this over the romantic meal I'm makin', but... Will you make me the envy o' every man in Atlanta by bein' my date to the Southern Comfort Ball this year?

LOLA. *What?*

ROBERT. I said. Ms. Lola Cola, I wanted to do this over the romantic meal I'm –

LOLA. I heard, I just... Oh Robert... I can't.

ROBERT. You already goin' with *Ms.* Miller?

LOLA. Stop it! No...it's just. All of you have gone so far. You've done so much to be who you are. But me... I mean, I'm still John when I pick up that phone.

ROBERT. But darlin'. SoCo ain't a place that don't accept you for that. Heck, it's one of the few places that *understands*.

LOLA. You talk like it's Heaven on Earth.

ROBERT. Don't sound so far off.

LOLA. It's a Sheraton Hotel and some rented event space. What's the big deal?

ROBERT. Hard to explain.

LOLA. Well, if it's so great there, why not just move to Atlanta?

ROBERT. What are you talkin' about?

LOLA. Just... Why are you living way out there where there's so much fear?

ROBERT. Cuz it's home. I got my land...with my tree on it.

> *(He is being somewhat silly, but* **LOLA** *is still noticeably concerned.)*

Look. If there are two things I know: One...I'm a man. And two...I'm a Toccoa man.

[MUSIC NO. 06 "SOUTHERN COMFORT"]

Not Augusta, not Atlanta. Toccoa.

LOLA. But sometimes the things you hear about out there. It just don't seem logical –

ROBERT. Logic ain't been on my side since the day I was born.

I GOT MUSIC ALL AROUND ME
IT'S BEEN SINGIN' ME SOMEWHERE
AND AS LONG AS IT STAYS WITH ME

I KNOW I'LL MAKE IT THERE.
IT'S NOT MY IMAGINATION
AIN'T NO WIND ACROSS A TREE
IF YOU TELL ME YOU DON'T HEAR IT
YOU AIN'T LISTENIN' PROPERLY.

IT'S THE SOUND OF ICE CUBES SINGIN' WHILE THEY'RE
SPINNING 'ROUND A GLASS
OR A BREEZE ALL FULL O' BARBEQUE YOU WISH WOULD
NEVER PASS
GETS YOU FEELIN' LIKE A CHILD IS ALL YOU BEEN ALL
    ALONG
SOUTHERN COMFORT'S WHAT THEY CALL IT
SOUTHERN COMFORT IS THE SONG

I COULD MOVE TO A BIG CITY
I COULD BLEND IN WITH THE CROWD
I COULD LOSE MY WAY IN BUSTLE
I COULD LOSE MY VOICE IN LOUD
BUT I WEREN'T BORN IN A CITY
I WAS BORN INSIDE MY SKIN
AND I AIN'T READY YET TO LEAVE IT
NOW I'M FIN'LLY SETTLED IN

IT'S A STORY THAT YOU HEARD BUT YOU STILL LISTEN
    WHEN IT'S TOLD
OR A PLACE YOU KEEP ON GOIN' CUZ IT'S NEVER GETTIN'
    OLD
AND YOU CRAVE IT LIKE IT'S WATER, LIKE IT'S
    EVERYTHING YOU BLEED
SOUTHERN COMFORT'S WHAT THEY CALL IT
SOUTHERN COMFORT IS ALL I NEED

IT'S MORE THAN SOME DANCE IN A RENTED BANQUET
    ROOM
OR SWAYING BACK AND FORTH TO A COUNTRY TUNE
IT'S MORE THAN US JUST PROVIN' WE AIN'T DOIN' THIS
    ALONE
OR COMIN' HOME SOMEWHERE THAT NEVER WAS OUR
    HOME
LIKE A PARKIN' LOT "HELLO"

STORYTELLERS.

HELLO HELLO

ROBERT.

FROM A STRANGER YOU MUST

ROBERT & STORYTELLERS.

FEEL LIKE YOU KNOW...

ROBERT.

...IT'S THE OPEN ARMS OF SOMEWHERE THAT IS NEVER
VERY FAR

IT'S A FEELIN' WE CAN FIND AGAIN JUST STANDIN' WHERE
YOU ARE

IN THE ONE WIDE OPEN PLACE WE AIN'T AFRAID TO FEEL

ROBERT & STORYTELLERS.

FREE

SOUTHERN COMFORT'S

ROBERT.

WHAT WE'LL CALL IT

AND BEFORE YOU'RE RID O' ME

ROBERT & STORYTELLERS.

SOUTHERN COMFORT'S

ROBERT.

WHERE I'M GOIN'

ROBERT & STORYTELLERS.

SOUTHERN COMFORT

ROBERT.

IS WHERE WE'LL BE

Scene Five (A): Summer / Transition to Scene Six

(Lights on the **STORYTELLERS.***)*

[MUSIC NO. 07 "SUMMER"]

ELIZABETH.

TIME IS HANGIN', DRENCHED AND WEARY
SATURATIN' EVERY TREE.
FRUIT ARE FILLIN' UP ITS BRANCHES
WITH THE WEIGHT OF MEMORY.
RIPE WITH LIVING,
BUT UNFORGIVING.
SUMMER'S MOVIN' IN ON ME

(Lights up on **MELANIE.***)*

MELANIE. Watchin' Robert get weak was like watchin' stone get soft...it just didn't make sense; at least not in the world I'd come to understand since meetin' Sam. Back then I was all kinds o' backwards: livin' in Mossy Acres Mobile Home Park, not talkin' to folk cuz o' the color o' their skin. Then I hear this rumor 'bout this woman who lives across the way – who isn't really a woman at all. Whew, Lord; the first time Sam showed up at my place I had a gun hid under the cushion o' my couch the entire time. Funny thing is, he was the first man in my life who I didn't need protectin' from. But when things got serious between us...well, we had to move from Mossy Acres...escape really.

ELIZABETH.

LOOK AT THE THUNDER RUN
LEAVIN' LIGHT ACROSS THE GREY

STORYTELLERS & ELIZABETH.

AND KEEP ON MOVIN'
MOVIN' AWAY

ELIZABETH.

NOTHIN' IS STANDIN' STILL
EVEN THE SKY WON'T STAY

STORYTELLERS & ELIZABETH.
IT KEEPS ON ROLLIN'
ROLLIN' AWAY

(Lights have expanded to reveal **SAM** *and* **JACKSON** *standing with* **MELANIE** *around the tree in Robert's backyard [as in the opening scene].)*

JACKSON. Lord, you were runnin' scared first time we met.

SAM. She thought y'all wouldn't accept her, not bein' like us n' all.

MELANIE. But Robert just took me right in.

(Touching **SAM.**)

Suddenly *we* had a home. A family. Without Robert, well...

ELIZABETH.
RIPE WITH LIVING,
BUT UNFORGIVING.
SUMMER'S MOVIN' US SOMEWHERE

STORYTELLERS.
SUMMER'S MOVIN' US SOMEWHERE

MELANIE. Guess we all came to this family in our own ways... I grew into it kind o' slow. But some of us came in with a bang.

(Lights up on **CARLY** *as she drops a bra on Jackson's table and moves into the scene with him.)*

Scene Six: Jackson's House

[MUSIC NO. 08 "PLACES THAT AREN'T EVEN THERE"]

(A spot on **JACKSON**; *in his underwear in bed. He preps a syringe as* **CARLY** *gives herself a shot with another syringe just above her buttocks.)*

CARLY. Hand me that cotton ball.

> (**JACKSON** *hands her a cotton ball, which she presses against the place on her skin where she has just administered the shot.)*

Mine dries out real quick.

JACKSON. Is yours as thick as mine?

CARLY. Estrogen is pretty thick.

JACKSON. Let me see.

CARLY. Show you mine if you show me yours.

JACKSON. Is that a promise?

CARLY. *Mr. Jack!*

> *(They trade syringes.)*

So, mine makes me irritable and yours makes you horny.

JACKSON. *(Moving in and touching* **CARLY**.*)* Well. Mine's workin'...

> WHEN YOUR HANDS ARE ON ME
> YOU TURN ME INTO SOMEONE WHO I WANNA BE
> SOMETHING IN YOUR FINGERS
> MAKES ME FEEL LIKE I'M NOT A MYSTERY
> YOU MAKE EVERY INCH OF ME
> AWAKE, AWARE
> TOUCHING ME IN PLACES THAT AREN'T EVEN THERE

LIZZIE & JOEL.

> YEAH YEAH
> YEAH YEAH
> YEAH YEAH YEAH

YEAH YEAH

(They kiss; it gets heated, then:)

JACKSON. *(Pulling away:)* Hey, uh –

So: they made me manager at work.

CARLY. *(Where's this going?)* O...kay.

JACKSON. And: I been thinkin'...with the new money I could be puttin' away – well, I might eventually be able to afford the surgery. You know. Not be half n' half.

CARLY. Is that what you want?

(A beat.)

JACKSON. I don't know. Robert's got strong feelings against it. But you...

That day we first met; before we started up. Remember; we were talkin' all about...

CARLY. *Sex.*

JACKSON. N' you said you always thought that one day; eventually, you knew you'd probably need a real...you know: *man.*

CARLY. I didn't say *man.*

JACKSON. No. But you did say...

CARLY. I also said someday. *Eventually.* So are we talkin' about gettin' married here, or –

JACKSON. No.

CARLY. Good. Then let's worry about what we want.

(Getting really close; touching him.)

Right. Now.

JACKSON. But, maybe I want to make you feel everything you want. Maybe I –

CARLY. *(Pulling him back into the fray.)* Shhh...

WHEN YOU MOVE INTO ME
I CAN FEEL EVERYTHING I WANNA BE
EV'RY MOVE YOU'RE MAKING
SOMEHOW MAKES THE TRUTH OF EVERY PART OF ME
NOTHING COMES BETWEEN US

NOT A BREATH OF AIR
YOU FILL ALL THE PLACES THAT AREN'T EVEN THERE

JACKSON & CARLY.

GO ON TAKE ME UNDER
ROLL ME LIKE THUNDER
BREAK ME ALL ASUNDER SO ALL I'LL BE
IS JUST PIECES OF A LOVER
ALL SCATTERED UNDER COVER
WHERE YOU'LL RE-DISCOVER EVERY PART OF ME

STORYTELLERS.

YEAH YEAH YEAH

JACKSON & CARLY.

TAKE ME LIKE A NEW WORLD
GO ON STRIP ME BARE
MOVE INTO MY BORDERS

JACKSON, CARLY & STORYTELLERS.

'TIL I'M SOMEPLACE WHERE
EVERY INCH IS FREE

STORYTELLERS.

YEAH YEAH

JACKSON, CARLY & STORYTELLERS.

FOR YOU AND I TO SHARE

JACKSON & CARLY.

TAKE ME TO

JACKSON, CARLY & STORYTELLERS.

THE PLACES

JACKSON & CARLY.

THAT AREN'T EVEN THERE

> (**JACKSON** *and* **CARLY** *crumble onto the bed,
> disappearing in the sheets. A moment, then
> we hear a knock.*)

JACKSON. Ah, shit.

CARLY. You expectin' someone?

JACKSON. Is it Sunday?

CARLY. Yeah.

JACKSON. I offered to host this monthly get-together we do.

CARLY. What?

> *(She jumps out of bed and throws on a robe.)*

Am I even supposed to be here?

JACKSON. Wasn't part o' the plan.

> *(Another knock.)*

CARLY. *(Moving cautiously into the kitchen, i.e. toward the front door.)* My bra is in the kitchen.

JACKSON. Oh, yeah.

> *(The door opens and* **ROBERT** *enters, followed by* **LOLA**, *just as* **CARLY** *enters the kitchen.)*

ROBERT. Hey Jack, it's –

> *(He notices* **CARLY**, *who stands like a deer in headlights, in Jackson's robe.)*

CARLY. Oh. Heya. Robert! Lola? I've heard so much! I'm Carly.

ROBERT. Who?

CARLY. Oh, um…

LOLA. Is this a bad time?

CARLY. *No!* Come in…

We were just…

> *(A moment.)*

I'm so sorry, I had no idea about any –

> *(Another moment.)*

Jackson! He's just…

ROBERT. Exhausted I bet.

> *(***JACKSON*** enters.)*

JACKSON. Hey Pops. Lola. Happy Sunday.

ROBERT. Jackson. We were just gettin' acquainted with…

LOLA. Carly.

JACKSON. You'll like her, Pops: She's real Holy-like. Used to be an altar boy n' everything.

CARLY. *Jack.*

JACKSON. Sorry, we're a lil' behind schedule.

LOLA. It's no big deal...

ROBERT. Well it's a big deal to me. You went t'all this trouble makin' a cake.

LOLA. It's Entenmann's.

CARLY. Ooo, my favorite!

LOLA. Thanks.

> *(An awkward moment of silence.)*

That's a nice robe. I love the color, it's so...watery. Which is perfect for a robe, you know?

CARLY. Thanks!

> *(Another weird moment...***CARLY** *grabs the cake from* **LOLA.***)*

I'll cut this up!

> *(Another knock at the door, and* **SAM** *and* **MELANIE** *enter.)*

MELANIE. Hey y'all, Happy Sunday!

SAM. *(To* **ROBERT.***)* You beat us!

MELANIE. *(Looking for a place to set a large bowl.)* Can I just plop this here on the –

> *(Taking notice of* **CARLY.***)*

Oh!

CARLY. Carly. Jack's friend.

JACKSON. *(To* **MELANIE***, as she sets down the bowl.)* Is that my favorite Snickers salad?

MELANIE. You n' everyone at my company picnic last week!

SAM. Not that I would know.

ROBERT. Mel, you still not invitin' Sam to those things?

MELANIE. Oh, he knows it ain't about him. The girls at my office...they're just nosey and ignorant. And their husbands are big and ignorant. A combination I don't much want to tempt.

JACKSON. Sounds like most o' Georgia you should be hidin' him from.

MELANIE. I ain't worried 'bout most o' Georgia – just the ones payin' my salary.

ROBERT. How 'bout this, I make it to SoCo, you take Sam here to your company Christmas party.

MELANIE. Hush, don't talk like that!

ROBERT. You didn't say "no."

(*Taking* **LOLA***'s hand:*)

Now all I gotta do is work out gettin' this one to go to Southern Comfort with me.

SAM. Y'all goin' together?

LOLA. No. No I…I'm not ready. Not this year.

MELANIE. (*Scooping the Snickers salad into bowls and passing it around.* **LOLA** *studies it, uncertainly.*) Speakin' o' SoCo; Sam, you're supposed to get that stuff from Jackson's garage, remember?

SAM. Oh yeah, I need those tools I lent you.

JACKSON. What's that got to do with SoCo?

SAM. I just been pickin' up some extra jobs; you know, makin' sure we can afford the trip.

JACKSON. Good luck findin' anything in there.

SAM. (*Exiting.*) Thanks, dude.

JACKSON. Oh hey, did y'all hear about Ralph Parker? Remember, lives in Fayetteville – sat at our table last year during the SoCo Ball? Word is he got himself a phalloplasty.

ROBERT. What a waste o' money.

CARLY. (*A sideways glance at* **JACKSON**.) I don't know, maybe not.

ROBERT. Jack maybe ain't mentioned: but we don't really buy into these ones sayin' you gotta have the surgery to be complete.

CARLY. Yeah, well, neither do I. No one should say you *gotta* do anything. But if someone thinks it's right for them, why not?

ROBERT. Well, it's a rip-off, one. They ain't got close to perfecting it, two. And it goes and reduces gender back to what's between the legs –

JACKSON. But Pops; why'd we start takin' hormones then? Why'd we get top surgery?

ROBERT. We gotta pass. But ain't no reason to put ourselves in the hands o' them Doctors any more than we need to. What's gotten into you?

(*An awkward beat.*)

CARLY. Well...uh, if you'll excuse me – I'm just gonna...get dressed.

LOLA. Oh, could you show me the restroom. I just have to powder my nose and then...

(*Setting down the Snickers salad as though glad to be rid of it.*)

...I'll be back for this.

(*They exit. An awkward moment.*)

JACKSON. She's uh... We met at SoCo the other year and kept in touch and –

ROBERT. We'd just appreciate a little warning – These Sundays are kind o' special and I didn't know we were... expanding.

JACKSON. I thought dates were okay now.

ROBERT. Lola ain't a date: She's family.

JACKSON. Not to me she ain't. I mean, what do we even know about her? She don't care to live anywhere near Taccoa. She ain't ever been to SoCo. She ain't even started on hormones yet.

ROBERT. Didn't know that was a prerequisite.

JACKSON. That ain't what I'm sayin'.

ROBERT. You're sayin' somethin'.

JACKSON. I'm sayin': Just cuz you think it don't make Lola part o' *us*, Robert. I mean; whose "Chosen Family" is this; ours or just yours?

ROBERT. Now that ain't fair. I been makin' every effort to be respectful bringin' in Lola. Seems like you're the only one with a problem.

JACKSON. Really? Melanie; you feel like Lola's your family?

MELANIE. I feel like she's a sweetheart.

JACKSON. Yeah, like a piece o' cotton candy. Full o' air.

MELANIE. Anyone need more salad?

JACKSON. And Lola won't even touch Mel's Snickers salad.

(*Trying to win* **MELANIE** *over.*)

She looked at it like it was a spider, right?

ROBERT. Well, if that's how we're definin' family; rules out Carly too.

JACKSON. I bet she takes a bite before Lola.

ROBERT. You bet?

JACKSON. I do.

ROBERT. Fine.

MELANIE. Fer gosh sakes.

LOLA. Sorry for disappearing. Carly n' I just got to talking "trade secrets" – she looks so darn good...

JACKSON. (*Grabbing the bowl of Snickers salad and handing it to* **CARLY**.) Not to worry. We kept this for you.

CARLY. Oh!

(**ROBERT** *lifts Lola's bowl off the table.*)

ROBERT. Lola's too!

JACKSON. (*Intercepting the bowl from* **ROBERT** *and bringing it to* **LOLA**.) I got it.

(*To* **LOLA** *as she takes the bowl from him.*)

Looks like throw-up, don't it?

LOLA. No. It looks beautiful.

(**LOLA** *and* **CARLY** *both push it around a bit; stealing a brief glance with one another. Then:*)

CARLY. *(Studying it.)* What's in it?

MELANIE. Snickers, green apples, cool whip and vanilla puddin'. But the secrets in the puddin'. It's gotta be instant!

LOLA. Mmm...

> *(LOLA moves it a bit closer to her mouth...still not sure. CARLY does the same. An awkward moment as everyone stares at them. LOLA lowers the spoon.)*

Carly, Do you live nearby, or...?

CARLY. *(Gladly lowering the bowl; setting it down and crossing away.)* Oh, no. I'm over in Augusta.

LOLA. Oh, yeah. We know that drive.

CARLY. *(To LOLA.)* You in Augusta?

ROBERT. I gotta doctor there.

> *(JACKSON has recovered CARLY's bowl and handed it back to her.)*

CARLY. Oh.

> *(A glance at the salad.)*

Why you go so far for the doctor?

LOLA.	**JACKSON.**
Well, it's the only one who'd –	We tried to find one closer but –

Sorry.

JACKSON. No harm. Just figured I'd answer since it happened way back before y'all knew each other.

> *(Egging on ROBERT.)*

Intimately.

ROBERT. Hey. Get Leprechaun here some more food, maybe he won't talk with a full mouth.

JACKSON. *(Taking a big bite and speaking with his mouth full – grossly.)* Lola, you want me to dump that out fer you?

LOLA. Oh, no, I...was just about...

> (**LOLA** *raises the spoon to her mouth...*
> *Everyone watches with anticipation...*)

...to...

> (*She looks back at them watching her...*
> *awkward.*)

I can't wait!

> (*All eyes remain on her. Finally, she takes*
> *a bite. Everyone cheers but* **JACKSON** *– who*
> *watches as his Chosen Family rallies around*
> **LOLA**.)

[MUSIC NO. 09 "CHOSEN FAMILY"]

LOLA.   **CARLY.**

What's goin' on?   What happened?

MELANIE. (*To* **LOLA** *and* **CARLY**.) Some dumb bet. C'mere;
y'all'll get used to it.

> (**MELANIE** *pulls* **LOLA** *and* **CARLY** *aside as*
> **ROBERT** *turns to* **JACKSON**.)

ROBERT. Well there you go, Jack. I know my girl.

JACKSON. Yeah, she's all that matters anymore.

ROBERT. Hey now. What's wrong with you today? Life's too
short for this kind of nonsense.

JACKSON. I know life's short, Robert. You don't gotta
remind me every god damn day.

> (**ROBERT** *turns toward* **JACKSON**, *who hastily*
> *exits the other way.* **CARLY** *follows* **JACKSON**
> *as* **MELANIE** *looks helplessly between the two of*
> *them, and lights fade on the scene.*)

Scene Seven: Sam & Melanie's House

> (**SAM** *is isolated in a spot of light, shaving.*
> *For a moment we simply watch him shave,*
> *then:*)

MELANIE. Jackson called fer you.

> (*Lights rise full to reveal* **MELANIE** *standing*
> *behind* **SAM**.)

Made a lot o' small talk 'til he finally got around to askin'
'bout Robert. Then Robert calls sayin' he needs some
car advice but suddenly askin' all kinds o' questions
about Jackson.

> (*A moment.*)

They still fightin'.

SAM. It'll blow over.

MELANIE. Well, you oughta just stay here this weekend
and we could have everyone over, make a little peace
between them.

SAM. They probably wouldn't agree to it anyhow.

MELANIE. I don't know. I never saw them get like that.
We could not tell 'em. Like that *Parent Trap* movie,
trick 'em into talkin' again! Ha ha, surprise!

SAM. Mel. Wouldn't make no difference, Robert's got his
parents comin' in this weekend.

MELANIE. Lord, Robert's got his parents comin' in, you're
goin' out to see yours. When did it become family week
in Toccoa?

SAM. Well...Robert's got his folks comin' in to tell 'em he's
sick. N' that just got me to thinkin'...

MELANIE. Yeah?

SAM. Well, I still owe Robert, for that loan he gave me to
start the business – when we needed to get out o' Mossy
Acres.

MELANIE. We're payin' him.

SAM. I know but...I just don't want to still owe him if...

Besides, last time we were over there, did you see his counter? Full o' envelopes with red showin' through the windows, so someone's after him for money.

MELANIE. So you're goin' home to ask for money? After all o' this time.

SAM. *(Splashing his face.)* How do I look?

> (**MELANIE** *crosses to him and touches his face.*)

MELANIE. Like a baby.

SAM. Well that's what I am, their baby.

MELANIE. You wouldn't know it the way they treat you. They call you Debbie. You gotta shave just so they'll let you in the door.

SAM. Yeah, well: Joke's on them.

MELANIE. Don't look like it.

SAM. Don't matter how it look:

[MUSIC NO. 10 "BLESS MY HEART"]

I COULD KEEP MY WHISKERS GROWIN'
JUST TO GET BENEATH THEIR SKIN
FIGHTIN' FIRE WITH THE FIRE THEY'RE TRYN'A SPREAD
I COULD ARM MYSELF FER BATTLE
BUT I WOULD RATHER WIN
BY SAYING WHAT MY MOTHER ALWAYS SAID:

SAM, LIZZIE, LIZ & JOEL.

IT'S ALL TALK
IT'S ALL CHATTER

SAM.

IT DON'T MATTER HOW IT SOUND
WHEN THEY SUM YOU UP BY JUST SOME OF YOUR PARTS

SAM, LIZZIE, LIZ & JOEL.

THROWING STONES

SAM.

IN GLASS PLACES

SAM, LIZZIE, LIZ & JOEL.

LEAVES NO TRACES TO BE FOUND
WHEN YOU TAKE THE HIGHER GROUND AND
BLESS THEIR HEARTS

(**SAM** *has given* **MELANIE** *a kiss goodbye;
she reluctantly smiles at his jovial attitude
toward it all as he exits.*)

LIZZIE, LIZ & JOEL.

OH, OH, OH BLESS THEIR HEARTS

(*Music continues as lights focus on...*)

Scene Eight: Jackson's House / Sam's Journey

> (*Lights up on* **JACKSON**, *who is looking through a box.* **CARLY** *enters as he pulls out an old baseball mitt.*)

CARLY. Uh-oh, this looks tragic.

JACKSON. (*Startled. Trying not to make too much of it.*) It's nothing. My dad sent this stuff over. Came across it cleanin' up and I guess he didn't want anything that reminded him o' me around.

> (**JACKSON** *lightly punches the mitt.*)

He used to love havin' a little girl who played ball with him...

> (*A beat.* **CARLY** *approaches* **JACKSON** *and sits beside him.*)

CARLY. Hey... Maybe you oughta give Robert a visit. You ain't been acting like yourself since you two stopped talkin'.

> (*Snapping out of the momentary emotional moment, putting the mitt away and closing up the box:*)

JACKSON. No way.

CARLY. But Jack; you gotta. So maybe he won't agree with you 'bout...what you're considerin'. But you two are more than that; I know it.

JACKSON. No one's more than that.

CARLY. That ain't true. Look at your dad. He sent that box. Maybe it seems like nothin'; but it is somethin'.
If you just reached out to him, showin' him who you are; I bet even he'd surprise you.

JACKSON. No deal. You say the truth. People disappear. That's people.

I COULD SPEND MY WHOLE LIFE LIVING
IN SOME STUPID KIND O' BLISS
LIKE I'LL CHANGE THE WORLD WITH SOMETHIN'

THAT I SAID
I COULD TRY TO MOVE A MOUNTAIN
OR I COULD SETTLE THIS
IN A PROPER SOUTHERN WAY INSTEAD

JACKSON, SAM, LIZZIE, LIZ & JOEL.

AND LET 'EM TALK
LET 'EM CHATTER

JACKSON & SAM.

NEVER MATTER ALL THE SOUND
WHEN THEY SUM ME UP BY JUST SOME OF MY PARTS

JACKSON, SAM, LIZZIE, LIZ & JOEL.

LET 'EM SHOUT
ALL ABOUT ME

JACKSON & SAM.

'TIL THEY DOUBT ME ALL AROUND
I'LL STILL STAND THE HIGHER GROUND
AND BLESS THEIR HEARTS

LIZZIE, LIZ & JOEL.

OH, OH, OH BLESS THEIR HEARTS

JACKSON, SAM, LIZZIE, LIZ & JOEL.

I CAN SEE THE WAY THEY'RE LOOKIN'
I CAN SEE WHAT'S IN THEIR EYES
LIKE THE GOOD LORD WROTE THE GOOD BOOK
JUST FOR THEM
BUT THEY'VE ONLY SEEN THE COVER
THEY AIN'T NEVER LOOKED INSIDE
THEY JUST LET THE PREACHER PREACH AND SING AMEN

LIZZIE, LIZ & JOEL.

AMEN
AMEN
AMEN
AMEN
AMEN

> (**JACKSON** *remains illuminated, but the focus returns to* **SAM.***)*

SAM.

IT'S ALL TALK

IT'S ALL CHATTER
IT DON'T MATTER HOW IT SOUND
JESUS PLEASE JUST HELP ME NOT TO FALL APART
STICKS N' STONES
NEVER BREAK ME
STILL, WORDS TAKE ME TO GROUND
EVEN WHEN THEY COME AROUND AND BLESS MY HEART

> *(Lights fade on **JACKSON**.)*

LIZZIE, LIZ & JOEL.

OH, OH OH BLESS MY HEART

> *(**SAM** takes a deep breath and moves toward his parents' house.)*

> *(**SAM** exits to face his family as lights cross-fade to **ROBERT**. A beat.)*

ROBERT. Hey, Ma. Dad.

> *(The **STORYTELLERS** playing **ROBERT'S PARENTS** are illuminated.)*

ROBERT'S MOTHER. Hello Barbara.

ROBERT'S FATHER. Hey there Barb, how you doin'?

ROBERT. I been better.

ROBERT'S MOTHER. Who was that we saw drivin' out when we came in?

ROBERT. That was Lola.

ROBERT'S MOTHER. Who's she?

ROBERT. She's my girl.

ROBERT'S FATHER. Is she a... I mean, *actually*...?

ROBERT. She's *actually* my girl. Nothin' else to it.

ROBERT'S MOTHER. ...I brought you a present.

> *(She holds out a small shoe box.)*

Just some old pictures I found o' you as a little –

ROBERT. Ma.

ROBERT'S MOTHER. Barbara –

ROBERT. Look at me. What did you tell your neighbors when I came to visit last? You call me Barbara then?

ROBERT'S FATHER. We say you're our nephew.

(*A stark spot illuminates the characters embodying the* **DOCTORS' VOICES.**)

DOCTOR'S VOICE 1. Ms. Eads. Our hospital is simply not equipped to deal with your...situation.

(**ROBERT** *shakes the voice off.*)

ROBERT'S FATHER. If they ask where our daughter is, I say, "Well, Barbara and I have had a little difference of opinion and we don't see much of her anymore."

DOCTOR'S VOICE 2. Perhaps you could try some place downtown? Ma'am?

ROBERT. (*Suddenly disoriented.*) Sir.

ROBERT'S FATHER. Excuse me?

DOCTOR'S VOICE 1. Have you tried Stephens County Hospital?

DOCTOR'S VOICE 2. Mountain Lakes Medical?

ROBERT. Please...

DOCTOR'S VOICE 1. My other patients would not be comfortable with our treatin'...someone like you.

DOCTOR'S VOICE 2. You may need to consider somewhere more urban like Augusta or Atlanta.

DOCTOR'S VOICE 1. I'm sure you understand.

DOCTOR'S VOICE 1.	**DOCTOR'S VOICE 2.**
Barbara.	Barbara.

ROBERT. *Robert.*

(**ROBERT** *stumbles a bit, then catches himself.*)

ROBERT'S MOTHER. Are you alright? Barbara?

ROBERT. Fine. I'm...fine.

ROBERT'S MOTHER. Wasn't there somethin' important you had to tell us?

ROBERT. No. There's nothin' to tell, I just: I wish you wouldn't call me Barbara.

(*Lights out on the* **DOCTORS** *and back to normal.*)

ROBERT'S FATHER. I had dreams that my daughter would grow up to marry a man who would become the President o' the United States or king o' some country. I knew that she was that kind o' a woman. And those dreams, as you well know, were shattered. Can't we at least call you by the name we gave you?

(Lights fade on **ROBERT'S MOTHER** *and* **FATHER.** *A moment as he looks at the box of photos left on the table. Finally, he crosses toward the box and lifts out a few of the photos within.)*

[MUSIC NO. 11 "BARBARA"]

ROBERT.

THERE'S BARB'RA
SWEET BARB'RA
WHO NEVER UNDERSTOOD
WHY SHE DIDN'T LIKE THE THINGS SHE SHOULD
AT TEA PARTIES ON SUNDAY SHE WOULD DITCH
ALL OF HER
TOYS
MRS. BEAR AND LITTLE SUE WERE NO MATCH FOR THE
BOYS
PLAYIN' HIDE AND SEEK OR BASEBALL OR JUST SLIPPIN'
THROUGH
A MESS
THEN COMIN' HOME TO TROUBLE FOR THE GRASS STAINS
ON
HER DRESS

[Projection: Christmas]

ROBERT & JOEL.

OH BARB'RA
POOR BARB'RA

ROBERT.	**JOEL.**
COME EVERY CHRISTMAS DAY	OH

ROBERT.

SHE COULDN'T WAIT TO GIVE HER TOYS AWAY

[Projection: Barbara holding a doll]

ROBERT.	JOEL.

ROBERT.

A PHOTO WITH HER DOLLY THEN   MM
OFF TO STRIKE A DEAL
AND CONVINCE HER LITTLE   OO
BROTHER HE WOULD MAKE OFF
WITH A STEAL:
THE DOLLY FOR A TELESCOPE, A HAIRBRUSH FOR A
BLADE
EVER SINCE SHE COULD REMEMBER SHE'D BEEN LOOKIN'
FOR A
TRADE

[Projection: Barbara on Easter]

ROBERT & JOEL.

THAT LITTLE GIRL ON EASTER
WAS A BOY STUFFED IN A DRESS

ROBERT.

WEARIN' LACE AND RUFFLES LIKE A GAG

ROBERT & JOEL.

SURE CHILDHOOD FOR EVERYONE
IS PAINFUL MORE OR LESS

ROBERT.

BUT FOR BARB'RA IT TRULY WAS A DRAG

ROBERT & JOEL.

SUCH A DRAG

AND BARB'RA
YOUNG BARB'RA
WOULD NEVER UNDERSTAND
HOW THE WORLD COULD HAVE A WHOLE LIFE PLANNED
OTHER FOLK COULD FOLLOW IT AND GLORY KNOWS SHE
TRIED
BUT THE TRUTH KEPT GETTIN' BIGGER 'TIL IT GREW TOO
MUCH
TO HIDE
STILL SHE WASN'T SCARED, SHE THOUGHT THE WORLD
WOULD
KNOW HER NOW BECAUSE
ALL THAT SHE WAS DOIN' WAS BECOMING WHO HE WAS

AND TO BARB'RA
SWEET BARB'RA
THE TRUTH WAS LIKE THE DAWN
BUT TO EVERYONE SHE'D EVER KNOWN

ROBERT.

BARB'RA WAS GONE

(Lights fade on the scene.)

Scene Nine: Robert's House / Jackson's House / Sam & Melanie's House

*(Lights on **CARLY**, who reads from a letter.)*

CARLY. Dear Patrick.

[MUSIC NO. 12 "LETTER INSTRUMENTAL"]

You don't know me, but I'm writing this letter in regard to your youngest child who you originally named Peggy Sue. And who I know as Jackson. I realize that you've been estranged from one another for close to ten years. I'm told that you do not take Jack changing his gender very well. I can assure you that your child is not a freak. Please just pick up the phone and call your son to say hello. Please tell Jackson that you love him even though you don't understand him. He is still your child.

*(**CARLY** extends her hand that holds the letter, and a member of the **STORYTELLERS** takes it, puts it into an envelope, and passes it down the line until it reaches the man playing **JACKSON'S FATHER**; he opens the letter and reads it as **CARLY** moves into the following scene, laying on the bed next to **JACKSON**. A moment, as **JACKSON'S FATHER** reads the letter. He removes a phone from his pocket and puts it to his ear.)*

JACKSON'S FATHER. Hi, are you there Jack? It's Patrick...uh... Dad.

*(**JACKSON** bolts upright.)*

I received the letter from your...friend and well. I'd appreciate it if you'd tell her or him or...whatever, to leave me out o' this. I don't need remindin' you're my child. I don't want nothin' to do with whatever you got goin' on. Okay. Bye Jack.

(A moment.)

JACKSON. Letter?

CARLY. I'm so sorry. I thought…maybe it would help. Maybe if he answered, you'd see that it would be okay to talk with Robert about… But, I'm so sorry, I had no idea he'd say –

JACKSON. He called me Jack.

CARLY. What?

JACKSON. He never called me Jack before, but in his message…

(Turning to CARLY, a smile on his face.)

What did you say to him?

CARLY. Oh, well. Just somethin' about how wonderful, amazin' his son is.

(Very close to him now, flirtatiously.)

So…

JACKSON. So?

CARLY. So maybe people don't always react exactly how you expect, even the ones you know the best.

JACKSON. Maybe.

CARLY. N' maybe it *is* better to just let 'em know you entirely before…you know.

(Lights cross-fade to LOLA standing in Robert's living room, an intimidating line-up of pill bottles in front of her. She reads the bottles as she makes notes in a small notepad.)

LOLA. Two of bottle one. One of bottle two…
One of bottle five only as needed, but not to exceed two in twenty-four hours.
Two of bottle seven twice a week –

(ROBERT enters. He walks unsteadily and is now using a cane. He also wears a baggy tuxedo jacket.)

ROBERT. *(Looking at the pill bottles, then pulling another one from his pocket and dumping some pills into his palm.)* More candy?

LOLA. *(Referring to the pills in his hand.)* Which one is that?

ROBERT. I don't know. What's it say?

> *(**LOLA** takes the bottle.)*

LOLA. It says:

> *(Reading, then glancing at his hand where he's dumped out the pills.)*

...not to take two.

ROBERT. I know. I only got...

> *(He looks in his hand.)*

Oh. That one must o' just fell out.

LOLA. *(Taking the extra pill and putting it back into the bottle.)* What're you wearin'?

ROBERT. Found my tux.

> *(Pulling at the baggy jacket.)*

I don't know...

LOLA. We'll get it altered.

ROBERT. I paid enough for it already.

LOLA. Don't worry; I know people.

ROBERT. Always fit me like a good glove.

> *(He pulls the jacket off and hands it to her. She folds it in her arms.)*

LOLA. Smells like that pipe.

ROBERT. *(Playing.)* Guess it must o' taken up smokin'.

LOLA. *(Through a reluctant smirk.)* Robert.

> *(A beat.)*

I got something to talk to you about.

ROBERT. You askin' me to SoCo? Cuz the answer's no. Too late.

LOLA. No, I want to –

ROBERT. I'm just kiddin', I'll go with you, fine.

LOLA. Robert! I wanted to ask...if you'll come live with me.

[MUSIC NO. 13 "MY LOVE"]

ROBERT. What?

LOLA. You heard me.

(Lights focus back on JACKSON and CARLY.)

JACKSON.

I'VE BEEN WRITIN' LETTERS IN MY HEAD SO LONG
EVERY SINGLE WORD I SAID JUST POURED OUT WRONG
IF I'D ONLY KNEW
ALL THE WORDS WERE THERE IN YOU

(Back to LOLA and ROBERT.)

ROBERT. I'd love nothin' more than to wake up next to you every day. But...I can't leave my home.

LOLA. Well...then, I'll come here.

ROBERT. I ain't gonna be no one's burden.

LOLA. Oh, you're so dramatic. I'm not askin' for your sake, I'm askin' for mine.

ROBERT. Way out here in Toccoa?

LOLA.

I'VE BEEN LIVIN' INSIDE WALLS WITH NO ONE THERE
JUST A BUNCH O' DOORS N' HALLS THAT GO NOWHERE
ONLY PLACES TO ROAM
BABY WON'T YOU BE MY HOME?

(Lights up on MELANIE as SAM enters and she lunges at him.)

MELANIE. You're *home*! Oh my god, I thought your family kidnapped you n' sent you to one o' them camps where they try to fix people who ain't broken.

SAM. Kidnapped? We talked every night.

MELANIE. It only takes an hour. They say they're takin' you to the Olive Garden and next thing you know – bam. Jesus jail!

SAM. *(Laughing.)* What're you talkin' about?

MELANIE. I don't know, I'm talkin' crazy!

(She kisses him all over his face.)

MELANIE. You okay? Did they...you know, help you out at all.

> (**SAM** *shakes his head "no."*)

Well...they treat you decent at least?

> (**SAM** *tries to respond, but can't. He crumbles into* **MELANIE**'s *arms and she cradles him, rocking him back and forth.*)

Shhh... You're perfect to me.

Every. Last. Inch.

IN MY EYES
YOU AIN'T ANY SORT A' RIDDLE
JUST FLESH AND BLOOD AND TRUE RIGHT TO THE MIDDLE

ALL & STORYTELLERS.

YEAH WHEN I'M WITH YOU I AIN'T STRANGE IN MY SKIN
I'VE NEVER BEEN QUITE SO AT HOME THIS FAR IN
IT'S LIKE I'M BEGINNING RIGHT BACK AT THE START
AND THE ONLY PART THAT'S TRUE
IS MY LOVE LOVE LOVE LOVE LOVE LOVE LOVE LOVE
LOVE LOVE
DRUMMIN' FOR YOU

LOLA. So...is that a yes? Roomy?

ROBERT. Depends.

LOLA. On?

ROBERT. You goin' to SoCo with me?

LOLA. *Blackmail!*

ROBERT. So...is that a yes?

LOLA. Well...

ROBERT. Well.

LOLA. Yes! Yes, yes, yes.

ALL & STORYTELLERS.

I'LL FOLLOW YOU UP AND RIGHT OVER THE AIR
TO TOUCH ALL THE PLACES THAT AREN'T EVEN THERE
WE'RE SPINNIN' IN SPACE SO FAR OFF OF THE GROUND
WHERE THE ONLY SOUND THAT'S TRUE
IS MY LOVE LOVE LOVE LOVE LOVE LOVE LOVE LOVE

LOVE
LOVE
DRUMMIN' FOR YOU

> *(Lights out on* **SAM** *and* **MELANIE**.*)*

JACKSON & CARLY.
MY LOVE

ROBERT & LOLA.
MY LOVE

STORYTELLERS.
DRUMMIN' FOR YOU

ROBERT & LOLA.
MY LOVE

STORYTELLERS.
DRUMMIN' FOR YOU

ROBERT, LOLA & STORYTELLERS.
MY LOVE MY LOVE (LOVE LOVE LOVE)

STORYTELLERS.
DRUMMIN' FOR YOU

> *(***LOLA** *and* **ROBERT** *kiss as* **JACKSON** *enters the scene.)*

JACKSON. Heya, Pops. Lola.

LOLA. Jackson.

JACKSON. Can I –

> *(***LOLA** *glances at* **ROBERT**.*)*

ROBERT. Sure...yeah. Come in.

LOLA. You boys want some tea?

ROBERT. I don't know...

LOLA. None of those flavors you hate, don't worry. I bought regular Lipton. I'll start some.

> *(She exits. A long silence;* **JACKSON** *takes* **ROBERT** *in. He doesn't look great.)*

JACKSON. You got a cane.

ROBERT. Fashion.

> *(A beat.)*

ROBERT. I haven't been able to get a hold o' you.
How's Carly? You ever get a chance to actually talk to her?

JACKSON. She's good, yeah. How 'bout Lola – She change the business to "Lola's Heatin' and Coolin'" yet?

ROBERT. She's comin' to stay with me.

JACKSON. *Here?* She's gonna be livin' here? Why?

ROBERT. Well, I'm needin' a little help.

(*Heavy beat.*)

She's goin' to Southern Comfort with me too!

JACKSON. Oh. Well... She and Carly can go get dresses together.

ROBERT. What's this? You actually making plans in advance with a girl?

JACKSON. Maybe.

ROBERT. Well praise God.

JACKSON. She's somethin' special. There, I said it – now let's never speak of it again.

ROBERT. My son's growin' up.

JACKSON. Pops.

ROBERT. I just hope she's more special than all the other special you known.

JACKSON. She wrote a letter to Patrick. My dad.

ROBERT. Yeah?

JACKSON. N' he called me n' –
Well, he didn't have much to say but, on the message, he called me Jack.

ROBERT. Well son, that's...

JACKSON. It's somethin'.

ROBERT. It's more than somethin'.

JACKSON. Yeah, and, it got me thinkin'... If he can call me Jack; well maybe you could... I don't know – maybe you –

ROBERT. What're you tryin' to say Leprechaun?

JACKSON. Well, I been thinkin' about it for a while but... now with my raise n' all at work... I may wanna be, you know, complete – n' get the surgery.

ROBERT. Be serious.

JACKSON. I am.

ROBERT. Just like that, you ain't even gonna talk with me about it?

JACKSON. You been busy with Lola.

ROBERT. What are you doin'?

JACKSON. What?

ROBERT. Why are you actin' like this? Every time I see you it's worse. Now you wanna fight about surgery?

JACKSON. I'm not fightin'. It's just...

(Sincere; trying.)

Remember what you told me: 'bout bein' my own man. Makin' commitments.

ROBERT. I was talkin' about an intimate commitment to someone else. Not goin' out o' your head. Not that your head's what you're thinkin' with.

JACKSON. Dammit, Robert. I am thinkin' with my head; my *own* head for once. Ain't got nothin' to do with Carly or –

ROBERT. Why all o' the sudden then? We *always* agreed that man or woman was about what's in your heart and your head, not between your legs. For ten years we *always* said –

JACKSON. Don't talk to me about ten years. Ten years, yeah, ten years o' you n' I sittin' on that front porch watchin' that tree grow, talkin' 'bout your little yard...your piece o' the world. And now Lola Cola's livin' here. And after you die, what then? She's just gonna stay on here, just take over your whole goddamn life –

ROBERT. Watch your mouth, son.

JACKSON. I ain't your son. And I ain't gonna watch my mouth cuz o' some God who don't give a shit about us.

Chosen Family? Like Hell, beggars can't be choosers, and if ever there was a group beggin' fer family –

ROBERT. I ain't ever begged for a family.

JACKSON. Are you kiddin' me?

ROBERT. What about you? You even try callin' your dad back?

JACKSON. You even tell your folks you're sick? Huh? You tell 'em where all your prayin's got you? All your beliefs? "Man and woman's just in your heart." Well your cancer sure ain't just in your heart, is it –

ROBERT. Why don't you just say what you wanna say about me.

JACKSON. Ain't about you, it's about –

ROBERT. Like Hell it ain't about me. You think what's happenin' to me – my cancer – is just Barbara eatin' me up inside cuz I ain't real. You think I –

JACKSON. I think I ain't makin' the same mistake you did. I ain't dyin' from bein' –

ROBERT. *Well I am*, Jack. Ain't nothin' gonna change that. I'm sorry if it's gettin' in the way o' your nonsense, but I –

JACKSON. *Christ, Robert!*

[MUSIC NO. 14 "I DON'T NEED ANOTHER FATHER"]

I DON'T NEED ANOTHER LECTURE
TO TELL ME HOW I'M WRONG
THIS AIN'T CHURCH AND IT AIN'T SUNDAY
I AIN'T HERE FOR KINGDOM COME
I JUST NEED A LITTLE QUIET NOW TO HEAR INSIDE MY
    HEAD
AND KNOW IT AIN'T JUST SAYIN' BACK THE THINGS YOU
ALWAYS SAID
I NEED TO KNOW THE PLACES WHERE YOU AIN'T A PART
    OF ME
BUT I DON'T NEED ANOTHER FATHER TO TELL ME WHO
    TO BE

I DON'T NEED ANOTHER PREACHER
TO PEDDLE SOME BELIEF
FROM A PAGE OUTTA THE GOSPEL
OF MR. ROBERT EADS
I JUST NEED A LITTLE MOMENT NOW TO LOSE MY FAITH
    AND FALL
N' CURSE A GOD WHO DOESN'T HEAR OR ANSWER TO MY
    CALL
I NEED TO DOUBT THE THINGS YOU DON'T FOR WHAT
    THEY DONE TO ME
NO I DON'T NEED ANOTHER FATHER TO TELL ME WHO TO
    BE

I BEEN DOWN THIS ROAD ALREADY
AND I KNOW WHERE IT GOES
IT DOESN'T MATTER IF THE FAMILY'S
SOMETHIN' THAT I CHOSE
SON OR DAUGHTER
BLOOD OR WATER; ANY WORD WE SAY
IT DON'T CHANGE THAT FAM'LY
ONLY GOES
ONLY GOES AWAY

> (**JACKSON** *turns to leave,* **ROBERT** *waivers –
> disoriented.*)

VOICE 1.	VOICE 2.	VOICE 3.	VOICE 4.
Barbara?	Barbara?	Barbara?	Barbara?
Barbara?	Barbara?	Barbara?	Barbara?
Barbara?	Barbara?	Barbara?	Barbara?

ROBERT. *(Shouting at the top of his lungs…)* ROBERT!

> (**JACKSON** *turns, startled.* **LOLA** *rushes into
> the room as* **ROBERT** *collapses;* **JACKSON** *looks
> on, horrified.*)

LOLA. What happened? Jack?

> (**LOLA** *looks back at* **JACKSON**, *who steps away
> and turns his back on the scene.*)

Jackson.

(Lights plunge to dark so that **JACKSON** *is illuminated in a spot.)*

JACKSON.
I DON'T NEED ANOTHER SOMEONE
TO HOLD ONTO MY HAND
UNTIL THE DAY I'M BRAVE ENOUGH
TO TELL'M WHO I AM
I DON'T NEED ANOTHER PERSON WHO MY WORLD CAN
SPIN AROUND
WHO GIVES ME FAITH IN SOMETHIN' THAT IS HIGHER
THAN THE GROUND
JUST TO LET ME GO AND DROP ME BACK TO WHERE I
USED TO BE
I DON'T NEED ANOTHER FATHER TO DISAPPEAR ON ME

(Another spot rises on **LOLA** *as she picks up the collapsed* **ROBERT** *and carries him offstage. Lights plunge to black.)*

End of Act One

ACT TWO

Scene One: Fall / Transition to Scene Two

(The **STORYTELLERS** *have been playing during intermission – or started playing near the end – an entr'acte that solidifies into the intro to "Fall.")*

[MUSIC NO. 15 "FALL"]

DAVID.

I NEVER REMEMBER IF YOU'RE COLD OR WARM
DON'T KNOW IF I'LL EVER DECIDE.
YOU GO BACK AND FORTH LIKE SOME KINDA STORM
THAT DON'T WANNA STICK TO A SIDE

LIZZIE.

BUT DON'T YOU REMEMBER HOW I CLUNG TO YOU
JUST WAVERIN' OUT IN THE SKY?
NOW HOW COULD YOU LET ME IF YOU ALWAYS KNEW
HOW QUICKLY WE'D TURN TO GOODBYE?

(Lights rise on all characters but **ROBERT** *– standing in the same positions as in the opening. The yard is transformed into Fall [as well as a representation of the Southern Comfort Conference] throughout the song.)*

ALL.

FALL AWAY

LIZZIE.

ALL IN A DAY WE START

JOEL.

SOON WE'LL BE THROUGH

AND ALL
ALL I CAN DO IS HOLD
HOLD ONTO YOU OR

ALL.

FALL
FALL

JOEL & LIZZIE.

BUT I STILL REMEMBER THE SMELL OF THE GREEN
SO HEAVY AND FULL IN THE AIR
WHEN LIFE WAS STILL LIVIN' AND NOT STUCK BETWEEN
THE STAYIN' AND GOIN' SOMEWHERE

LOLA. We skipped the Sunday get-together that month... what with Robert in the hospital n' all. Everyone just visited on their own time...

CARLY. Almost everyone.

ALL.

LEAVE LET GO

ELIZABETH.

WE'VE GROWN TO GROW APART

DAVID.

AND MAYBE IT'S TRUE
BUT ALL
ALL I CAN DO IS HOLD
HOLD ONTO YOU OR

ALL.

FALL

LOLA. We skipped Sunday the next month too.

SAM. There was no point, really.

MELANIE. It just didn't seem right; not without...you know, everybody.

LIZZIE.

DO YOU EVER MISS THE PLACES
WHERE WE USED TO BE ATTACHED?

DAVID.

ARE THERE EVEN ANY TRACES THAT ARE STRONG
ENOUGH TO LAST?

JOEL.

IS IT BETTER TO ERASE US

IF THERE'S NOTHING LEFT TO GRASP

ALL.

WILL I ONLY SPIN IN SPACE

ELIZABETH.

UNTIL I LEAVE YOU IN THE PAST...

ALL.

...AND FALL AWAY

LIZZIE.

ALL IN A DAY I'LL START

ALL.

LEAVE, LET GO

LIZZIE & JOEL.

WE'VE GROWN TO GROW APART

AND ALL

YES ALL I CAN DO

IS LET GO

LET GO OF YOU AND

ALL.

FALL

FALL

FALL

FALL

> *(The yard is transformed into an autumnal*
> *palate. A spot on **SAM**.)*

SAM. Southern Comfort, Atlanta. The cotillion of the transgender community. Ain't nothin' like it, not on this whole green earth. SoCo's where I first met Robert. I remember I had finally built up the nerve to come one year but...the second I got to my hotel room, I couldn't leave. I was horrified. For so long I'd been tellin' myself that once I got here it would be different, I'd be totally understood. And then suddenly I'm in my room thinkin', "Damn, what if they don't understand me either?" But Robert was down the hall o' that hotel knockin' on doors lookin' for anyone hidin' in a corner or scared to come out. The second I opened my door and saw'm standin' there it was like...I knew him. He was a complete stranger, but – he reached out his hand and said, "Welcome home." And I knew it was true.

Scene Two: The Southern Comfort Conference (SoCo) – Lobby

(*Lights up to reveal* **LOLA** *and* **MELANIE**, *along with* **SAM**. **LOLA** *looks around the lobby in amazement.*)

LOLA. I can't believe it...everywhere you look. I mean, for once we're not outnumbered.

SAM. Welcome home Ms. Lola Cola.

MELANIE. I just wish we all could o' been here.

(**LOLA** *snaps out of her awe.*)

Sorry. I know we said we wouldn't talk about...

I just can't believe he's not here. I really believed we'd all be here together.

SAM. Me too.

(*A moment, then* **ROBERT** *enters.*)

ROBERT. Okay, I worked my magic and we're on the same floor together – with a view o' the finest parkin' lot in Atlanta!

(*Everyone tries [badly] to cover what they've just been discussing. They stare at* **ROBERT** *and then between one another...as though they've been caught in the act.*)

What's goin' on?

LOLA.	SAM.	MELANIE.
We were just admiring the décor.	Just sorting out dinner.	Lola was just telling me about her dress

ROBERT. Y'all are talkin' 'bout Jackson already?

(*A guilty beat.*)

Well, he'd be thrilled we're givin' him the satisfaction.

LOLA. Robert –

ROBERT. I'm just sayin' – We're at SoCo, let's not act like it's a funeral. You'll have one o' those soon enough –

MELANIE. *Hush with that talk!*

ROBERT. I'm sorry –

>   *(Suddenly, from offstage:)*

CARLY. *(Offstage.) Melanie??*

MELANIE. *(Looking around, confused – almost panic.)* Who's that?

CARLY. *(Entering from offstage.)* Sam! Lola! Hey!

MELANIE. *(Relieved.)* Carly!

LOLA. Hey darling!

CARLY. Oh my God, it feels like forever. How are y'all?

>   *(Seeing* **ROBERT** *– noticeably moved.)*

> Robert!

>   *(She lunges at him and pulls him into a big hug.)*

> You look like a gazillion dollars.

ROBERT. Must not be worth what it used to.

>   *(They laugh – a moment.)*

CARLY. Did...uh... Is Jackson with y'all?

LOLA. *(Putting a supportive hand on* **ROBERT.***)* No. After the things he said to Robert –

ROBERT. We fell out o' touch a little.

SAM. A lot.

ROBERT. We thought he'd be with you.

CARLY. No we... Well – he fell out o' touch with me too.

ROBERT. *(He didn't expect that.)* Oh.

>   *(A quiet, tense moment.)*

MELANIE. Well you look just beautiful, don't she?

CARLY. Finally. I was wonderin' when someone was gonna say it!

>   *(They laugh.)*

> Hey, what are y'all doin' tonight?

ROBERT. Just settlin' in. Maybe we'll see what kind o' stuff they got goin' on before dinner.

CARLY. Well...

> *(Pulling some pamphlets out of her purse and handing them to everyone.)*

Can I interest any o' you in this?

LOLA. "Sensual Feminine Movement": a seminar moderated by...

> *(Looking up at* **CARLY.***)*

This is you!

MELANIE. Well, well. Moderating your own seminar at Southern Comfort!

CARLY. *(Jokingly.)* Want an autograph?!
Seriously though, I'd love to have some familiar faces in the crowd.

LOLA. Oh. I think this year will be more sidelines for me.

MELANIE. C'mon, it sounds like fun. And I could use a few pointers myself.

LOLA. I don't know.

ROBERT. C'mon, we'll all go.

LOLA. You?

SAM. Why the heck not. Nothin' wrong with gettin' in touch with our feminine sides, right?

ROBERT. A lil' boys' and girls' night out. What d'ya say?

LOLA. I just don't think –

CARLY. Oh, *please* Lola! It would mean the whole world to me if you were there.

LOLA. Well...how can I say no to that?

ROBERT. Alright. Now what're we still hangin' 'round here for? Let's drop off these bags and get goin'.

> *(Music begins as lights go out on all but* **CARLY.***)*

Scene Three: SoCo – The Passing Seminar

(**CARLY** *stands facing the audience – isolated in a pool of light.*)

[MUSIC NO. 16 "WALK THE WALK"]

CARLY. Well hey there, thanks for comin'! This here is Sensual Feminine Movement and if you're here, you're lookin' for some pointers on how you can better embody your true gender – instead o' the one that everyone around you was always trainin' you to be while you were growin' up.

(*Lights rise to reveal* **LOLA**, **MELANIE**, **ROBERT**, *and* **SAM** *facing out and watching* **CARLY** *as she leads the seminar.*)

Remember we have varying degrees of folk here in all different stages of transition; so just follow along, or watch. And like anything here at SoCo, take it at your own pace and just enjoy, okay?

LET'S MAKE BELIEVE WE'RE BACK IN GENESIS
WHERE ELSE TO BEGIN?
WITH ADAM HALFWAY TO LOSIN' BLISS
YOU GOTTA SELL
YOU GOTTA SELL SOME SIN

CUZ WICKED FRUIT HANGIN' FROM A VINE
IT DON'T MOVE SO WELL
BUT PUT A LITTLE SNAKE INTO YOUR SPINE
AND YOU CAN RAISE SOME HELL

CUZ A GIRL AIN'T WHAT SHE'S WEARIN'
AND A BOY AIN'T HOW HE'S BORN
YOU'RE THE MOVES YOU MAKE N' THEY GOTTA TAKE YOU
PAST THE THINGS YOU'VE WORN
CUZ WHAT A BODY IS OR NOT
IS JUST A WHOLE LOTA TALK
YOU GOTTA WALK THE WALK
OH OH OH OH
YOU GOTTA WALK THE WALK

*(Lights reveal **JACKSON** in a hospital gown. As the **DOCTOR** moves toward him:)*

DOCTOR. *(Looking at some files.)* Alright, now. The clinic just requires that you complete this paperwork.

JACKSON. All o' this?

DOCTOR. That's right.

*(A beat as **JACKSON** flips through the large stack.)*

You are aware that insurance won't cover this?

JACKSON. Yes.

DOCTOR. You're comfortable with the cost, then?

JACKSON. Yes.

*(Focus back on **CARLY**.)*

CARLY.
GOTTA CENTER GRAVITY ON YOUR HIPS
KEEP YOUR SHOULDERS BACK
A TILTED HEAD AND POUTIN' LIPS
BUT KEEP YOUR NECK RELAXED

NOW MOVE THE WAY THAT WATER FLOWS
NEVER IN A LINE
JUST THINK IN CURVES DOWN TO YOUR TOES
AND

CARLY & STORYTELLERS.
THEN BACK UP YOUR SPINE

*(Focus back on **JACKSON** and **DOCTOR**.)*

DOCTOR. I understand we're just doing some preliminary tests to make sure you're healthy enough to go through with the surgery? When the time comes.

*(**JACKSON** nods.)*

But when the time does come; you're familiar with the procedure?

JACKSON. More'r less, yeah.

CARLY (ROBERT, SAM, MEL & LOLA).
YOU CAN SPEND YOUR DAYS IN A MIRROR

(OH OH OH YEAH YEAH YEAH)
YOU CAN SPEND YOUR DOUGH ON SUPPLIES (OH)
BUT WITHOUT ALL THE MOVES THEY'LL JUST SAY IT
    PROVES
YOU'RE ONLY IN DISGUISE
CUZ WHAT A BODY IS OR NOT
IS A WHOLE LOTA TALK
YOU GOTTA WALK THE WALK
OH GOTTA WALK GOTTA WALK OH OH OH

DOCTOR. We'll graft the skin from here…

> *(He takes **JACKSON**'s arm and runs his finger down his forearm.)*

…on your arm.

JACKSON. Will it scar?

DOCTOR. There will be a relatively large scar, yes.

JACKSON. Right there on my arm? For everyone to see? Can't you take it from somewhere else?

DOCTOR. That's the way we do it. Now, there's also a chance that the arm's function may be hampered. But that's the least of your worries – the major risks involve the phalloplasty itself.

CARLY.

WE WEREN'T BORN WITH DEFINITIONS
WE WERE SLATES AND WE WERE CLEAN
WE JUST FOLLOWED THEIR INSTRUCTIONS
AND GREW INTO THE SAME ROUTINE
NOW IF WE MISS EVEN THE GIST
OF A TWIST UPON THE WRIST
WE CAN RISK OUR WHOLE EXISTENCE IN BETWEEN

ALL.

CUZ YOU CAN'T HIDE UNDERNEATH YOUR CLOTHING
YEAH YEAH YEAH
WE'RE ALL MEASURED IN A GLANCE OH
IN A SINGLE LOOK YOU'RE AN OPEN BOOK UNLESS YOU
    LEARN
THE DANCE
YOU LEARN THE DANCE

YOU LEARN THE DANCE

> *(Dance break in which each group cycles through the motions. The dance continues, during which* **ROBERT** *and* **SAM** *jokingly switch "gender movements," etc. The dance bleeds into* **JACKSON**'s *scene, so that the characters are moving through the* **DOCTOR**'s *office (during the following lines) – their joyous comradery a stark contrast to* **JACKSON**'s *sterile/isolated environment...)*

DOCTOR. Are you okay?

JACKSON. I'm alright...just... You know, it's a lot.

DOCTOR. Usually people bring someone along. Particularly to the actual procedure. If there's no one you know who's...comfortable with that, I have a list of volunteers who –

JACKSON. No I... I'll be okay.

CARLY.	EVERYONE ELSE.
YOU GOTTA WALK THE WALK OH	OH
	GOTTA WALK GOTTA WALK
OH OH OH YOU GOTTA WALK THE WALK OH	OH OH OH
	OH
	GOTTA WALK, GOTTA WALK
OH OH OH WALK THE WALK	OH OH OH
	WALK WALK WALK THE WALK
GOTTA WALK THE	
	GOTTA WALK
OH OH OH YOU GOTTA WALK THE WALK OH	OH OH OH
	WALK WALK WALK THE WALK

GOTTA WALK GOTTA
WALK

OH OH OH

OH OH OH

YOU GOTTA WALK THE WALK

YOU GOTTA WALK THE
WALK

(The groups continue to dance as a spot focuses on **LOLA**, *who moves with more and more confidence and with a big smile on her face. She continues to follow the movements as the scene changes to...)*

Scene Four: The Flower Shop / Lola's Room

(**LOLA** *remains illuminated in the spot as* **ROBERT** *moves center and speaks out.*)

[MUSIC NO. 17 "FLOWER SHOP INTERLUDE"]

ROBERT. I need...the most lovely flowers you've got. You make corsages?

(*Lights reveal one of the* **STORYTELLERS** *portraying the* **FLORIST.**)

FLORIST. Of course! What sort of complexion is the lady?

ROBERT. Beautiful.

(**LOLA** *becomes animated and pulls her dress out of the closet.*)

FLORIST. I see. I don't suppose you know the color of her dress?

(**LOLA** *holds the dress up to herself, then lays it out in preparation for the ball.*)

ROBERT. Midnight blue.

FLORIST. Well what an amazing date you are, knowin' the color o' her dress. If only all the men in this world were more like you.

ROBERT. I couldn't agree more.

FLORIST. What's the occasion?

ROBERT. The prom that never happened.

My girlfriend never got to go to her prom so tonight they're havin' a kind o' prom for folk who didn't get to go, and I'm takin' her to it.

FLORIST. How lovely.

She sounds real special.

(*The* **FLORIST** *hands* **ROBERT** *a corsage.*)

ROBERT. Oh yes. She's the most beautiful flower I could'a asked for. And she's still bloomin' more each day...

LOLA. *(Humming happily/absentmindedly as she studies herself in the mirror...liking what she sees.)*
    LALALA
    LALALA
    LALA LA LA LA
    LALALA
    LALALA
    LALA LA LA LA

       (Lights fade on the scene as they rise on...)

Scene Five: SoCo – Sam & Melanie's Hotel Room

> *(Spots illuminate **SAM** and **MELANIE**, both putting the finishing touches on themselves.)*

MELANIE. *(As she gets herself ready.)* Sam.

> *(A beat as she considers her question.)*

How's Robert seem to you?

SAM. Considerin' he could barely walk last month, I think he's –

MELANIE. No, I mean; bein' here without Jackson n' all.

SAM. Oh.

Well; I think Lola bein' here helps a lot.

But...he's crushed. He's gotta be.

MELANIE. And what about you; you okay?

> *(A beat. **SAM** turns to **MELANIE** as he straightens his tie; changing the subject.)*

SAM. This look alright?

> *(Lights expand on the entire scene as **MELANIE** turns to him.)*

MELANIE. *(Crossing to him.)* Tie's crooked.

> *(She reaches up and starts straightening his tie. **SAM** recoils a bit when her hand comes in contact with his chest.)*

SAM. Sorry.

MELANIE. Sam. What's wrong? You been over that for ages.

> *(He presses his hand to the spot she's touched; no response.)*

You know plenty o' men got much worse scars on their chests. Men who ain't even had surgery.

SAM. I know it. It's just...ever since those things Jackson said to Robert...

MELANIE. Yeah?

SAM. Feels like... I don't know. Like you're touchin' me down to who I used to be... Like it reminds you that I...

MELANIE. *Stop right there!*

> *(**MELANIE** crosses to her suitcase and starts digging through it.)*

I was gonna do this later, but –

> *(She pulls out a small box and crosses back to him.)*

Here.

SAM. I didn't know we were doing gifts.

MELANIE. *We* aren't, now hush up n' just open it.

> *(He opens up the box and pulls out a tie.)*

SAM. A tie.

> *(**MELANIE** beams.)*

It's nice. But...

MELANIE. *(Rude!)* But?!

SAM. Well... I just... I don't know that it's right for the SoCo Ball. It's got Christmas trees all over it.

MELANIE. It ain't for the ball, silly. It's for my company Christmas party.

[MUSIC NO. 18 "I'M WITH YOU"]

SAM. For me?

MELANIE. 'Bout time them fools see what a real husband looks like.

I'M DONE WITH THE GIRL FROM MOSSY ACRES
I DON'T WANNA BE THAT GIRL NO MORE
WATCHIN' MY BACK EVERY STEP I'M TAKIN'
DON'T KNOW WHAT I'M EVEN LOOKIN' FOR

I'M DONE WITH YOU NEEDIN' TO BE PATIENT
WATCHIN' ME TAKE EVERYTHING SO SLOW
I'M WORN OUT FROM STANDIN' IN ONE PLACE AND
NOW THERE'S ONLY ONE PLACE LEFT TO GO

SO SOUND THE ALARM

WE'RE GOIN' ARM IN ARM
AIN'T NO OTHER THING I'D RATHER DO
DON'T REALLY CARE
WHO MIGHT STOP N' STARE
BABY YOU'RE MY MAN AND I'M WITH YOU

I'M DONE WITH JUST BRINGIN' SNICKERS SALAD
NOW I'M BRINGIN' YOU ALONG WITH ME
CUZ LIFE AIN'T FOR FEEDIN' ALL THEIR HABITS
IT'S FOR BEIN' WHO WE GOTTA BE

SO LET THEM ALL LOOK
WE'RE AN OPEN BOOK
TAKE MY HAND AND MAKE IT IN PLAIN VIEW
RIGHT BY MY SIDE
NOTHIN' LEFT TO HIDE
BABY YOU'RE MY MAN AND I'M WITH YOU

WELL HONEY IT AIN'T NOTHIN' TO BE SO EXCITED FOR
GREEN PUNCH ON THE TABLES AND FAKE SNOW ON THE
    FLOOR
GOSSIPIN' 'BOUT STRANGERS LIKE IT ISN'T ALL A BORE,
    MMM
NEXT YEAR YOU'LL BE LOOKIN' TO GET FREE
BUT BABY TOUGH LUCK, YOU'RE STUCK WITH ME

MELANIE.	SAM.
SO BEG SCREAM N' SHOUT	
	NO NO NO NO
THERE AIN'T NO WAY OUT	NO WAY OUT
YOU ARE MY PLUS ONE AND WE	YOU ARE MY PLUS ONE
MAKE TWO	
	WE MAKE TWO
PLEASE UNDERSTAND	
WE GO HAND AND HAND	WE GO HAND AND HAND
BABY YOU'RE MY MAN	BABY BABY
	I'M YOUR MAN
MY MAN	YOUR MAN

BOTH.
AND THEY'LL WONDER WHY

AFTER TIME GOES BY
AFTER ALL THIS NONSENSE IS LONG THROUGH
WHY ALL THE FUSS
OVER FOLK LIKE US?

MELANIE.   **SAM.**

WHEN WE AIN'T SAYIN'
NOTHIN' ALL THAT NEW
JUST BABY YOU'RE MY MY MAN
MY MAN

                    BABY I'M YOUR MAN
                    YOUR MAN

BABY YOU'RE MY MAN
MY MAN

                    BABY I'M YOUR MAN
BABY YOU'RE MY MAN   BABY I'M YOUR MAN
AND I'M WITH YOU   AND I'M WITH YOU

(Lights fade on **SAM** *and* **MELANIE** *as they rise on...)*

Scene Six: SoCo - Robert's Hotel Room

(**ROBERT** *stands in his tux. A moment, and then* **LOLA** *emerges from the restroom – dressed in her gown and looking radiant.*)

ROBERT. Praise Jesus. You're amazin'.

LOLA. So're you.

ROBERT. But...it's missin' somethin'.

LOLA. (*Looking herself over.*) What?

(*He reveals the corsage.*)

Oh. It really is...my prom.

(*She slips it on.*)

Is that right?

ROBERT. I think. Actually.

LOLA. My mother never taught me.

ROBERT. There. Now you're complete.

LOLA. Almost.

(*She reaches into her purse and pulls out a pair of earrings, which she holds up to her ears.*)

What do you think?

ROBERT. I want my body to be cremated.

LOLA. Okay, I'll try another pair.

ROBERT. I'm serious.

LOLA. Well...what do you want me to... What I am supposed to –?

ROBERT. I just need to make sure someone knows all o' this. And I need it to be you.

(**LOLA** *sits down.*)

Afterwards, once you have the ashes –

LOLA. (*Getting up again.*) Robert, I... I don't know if I'm strong enough for this.

ROBERT. You're the only one I got left strong enough for this. N' in heels to boot. And it's just beautiful.

LOLA. You are... You're so...

ROBERT. Don't say cute!

> (**LOLA** *laughs and he moves to chase her.*)

Cuz what have I said about –

> (**ROBERT** *stops suddenly and braces himself on a chair.*)

LOLA. Are you okay?

ROBERT. Fine. Just all that...hoopla goin' out flower huntin'...and...

LOLA. Maybe we should take it easy tonight. Just...have our own little prom right here in the room.

ROBERT. Don't be silly.

LOLA. But...you're exhausted and you don't want to push it so hard that you...

> (*A moment.*)

I mean...what's the point to go all the way downstairs? We can dance right here. We're already all dolled up! We've got the radio, we can just turn on the tunes and –

> (**ROBERT** *takes her hand and raises his finger to his lips [i.e. "shhh"].*)

[MUSIC NO. 19 "I'M GOIN'"]

ROBERT.

> I AIN'T GOIN' FOR DANCIN'
> STILL I'LL DANCE ON AIR
> I DON'T GO TO DRESS UP
> BUT, HEY, LOOK WHAT I GET TO WEAR
> NOW I AIN'T TRY'N TO SHOW OFF
> BUT WHEN I WALK IN WITH YOU
> NOT BEIN' NOTICED WON'T BE WHAT I'M GOIN' TO DO
>
> I DON'T GO FOR FLOWERS
> BUT THEY SURE SMELL SWEET
> I AIN'T THERE FOR MUSIC
> BUT WHEN I HEAR THE BEAT
> I HOPE YOU'LL EXCUSE ME

CUZ UNTIL THE NIGHT'S THROUGH
LETTING YOU GO WON'T BE WHAT I'M GOIN' TO DO

OH DARLIN' I'M GOIN' TO TURN US N' TURN US 'TIL WE
    START TO SWAY
'TIL LIFE'S ALL A BLUR AROUND US AND WE LOSE OUR
    WAY
AND NOBODY STARES
LIKE WE'RE IN DISGUISE
OR WHISPERS OUT PRAYERS
WHEN THEY REALIZE
CUZ NOBODY CARES
WE AIN'T LIVIN' OUT LIES
NO NO NO

I AIN'T GOIN' FOR DANCIN'
BUT I'M GONNA DANCE
AIN'T GOIN' TO CHEAT DEATH
BUT IF I STAND A CHANCE
I'LL SPEND EVERY SECOND
JUST LIKE THIS WITH YOU
CUZ TOO MUCH LIVIN' GETS WASTED
ON NOT BEIN' TRUE
AND DARLIN' I'M GOIN'
YEAH, DARLIN' I'M GOIN'
DARLIN' I'M GOIN'
DARLIN' I'M GOIN'
BUT GOIN' AIN'T ALL THAT I'M GOIN' TO DO
MM MM

      (**ROBERT** *spins* **LOLA** *around the room as the*
      scene changes to...)

Scene Seven: SoCo – The Ball

(**LOLA** and **ROBERT** continue to dance as lights shift to reveal **SAM** and **MELANIE** also dancing.)

[MUSIC NO. 20 "MY LOVE (REPRISE)"]

DAVID.

> I BEEN DROWNIN' IN YOUR GLANCES ALL NIGHT LONG
> SWIMMIN' THROUGH THESE DANCES TRYIN' TO BE STRONG

DAVID & ELIZABETH.

> BUT THE WEIGHT OF YOUR STARE
> DON'T GIVE ME A BREATH OF AIR

MELANIE. (To **ROBERT** and **LOLA**.) Don't this place look amazin'?

SAM. It's beautiful.

ROBERT. (To **SAM** and **MELANIE**.) Hey, so's that tie, there!

(**CARLY** enters. **LOLA** notices her and waves.)

CARLY. (Crossing to the group.) Look at y'all. Lola, you look ready for the red carpet.

LOLA. You too.

CARLY. Thanks. I can't breathe.

MELANIE. Hey, go set your stuff at our table before some weirdo sits with us!

(**CARLY** laughs, moves over to their table, and sits down. She watches "the band" as they continue to sing.)

ELIZABETH.

> I BEEN HOLDIN' ONTO YOU LIKE YOU WERE LAND
> SCARED TO LET AN INCH OF YOU SLIP THROUGH MY HAND

DAVID & ELIZABETH.

> IF I LET GO OF YOU
> DON'T KNOW HOW I'LL MAKE IT THROUGH

CARLY.

> I GET THINKIN' 'BOUT YOU EVERY NOW AND THEN
> JUST A LITTLE WHISPER ASKIN' HOW YOU BEEN
> NOTHIN' I WON'T GET THROUGH

CARLY & ELIZABETH.

> THAT'S JUST GETTIN' OVER YOU

> *(LOLA takes notice of CARLY watching "the band." She whispers into ROBERT's ear, then:)*

ROBERT. *(To CARLY.)* Hey, how 'bout I give my princess a break and take a turn with you.

CARLY. No, y'all should be dancin' tonight, I'm not gonna –

SAM. Lord knows my two left feet'll welcome a break. Lola can have Mel.

MELANIE. *(Jokingly.)* Do I get any say?

SAM. Nope.

MELANIE. *(To LOLA, as she grabs her away from ROBERT.)* Lucky thing you're pretty.

> *(LOLA and MELANIE have an awkward moment as they try to figure out who should put their hands where [i.e. who should lead].)*

I grabbed you, so...you're the girl.

LOLA. I'll try!

> *(They laugh and begin to dance... Lights focus on CARLY and ROBERT.)*

ROBERT. You miss him?

CARLY. Who?

ROBERT. Like I gotta say. Me too.

> *(A moment.)*

I thought for sure he'd be here with you.

CARLY. Oh come on. You know Jack better than that.

ROBERT. Well: I know 'm enough to know that the real question is: Are you gonna take the deadbeat back once he comes to his senses?

CARLY. *(With a laugh.)* You think he will?

ROBERT. I give'm 'til Christmas. He ain't never missed a tree trimmin' in my backyard. And he 'specially won't with you bein' there.

CARLY. Me?

> *(Touched by the invite.)*

You're too sweet.

> *(A beat as they dance. **CARLY**'s smile fades.)*

I don't understand. I kept askin' him what happened; why he wasn't goin' to see you in the hospital...

> *(A beat. **CARLY** is getting upset.)*

You two were everything to each other. How could somethin' like surgery change that?

ROBERT. Wasn't about that. We just...

We hit somethin' we didn't know how to face, and – well –

> *(Overcome with sudden emotion; he struggles against it.)*

I don't blame Jack for bein' scared.

> *(He is struggling.)*

CARLY. Oh, Robert. I'm sure if you just talk to Jackson –

ROBERT. Nah. Time's the only thing. No forcin' it.

CARLY. But, Robert.

[MUSIC NO. 21 "CHOSEN FAMILY (REPRISE)"]

ROBERT.
NOT ANOTHER WORD
NOT A WHISPER 'BOUT TOMORROW
OR A QUIVER ON THE LIPS THAT BRINGS BACK
    YESTERDAY
WE'RE JUST DANCING NOW
ON A DAY GOD LET ME BORROW
SO JUST SETTLE INTO NOW AND WE CAN STAY
WHERE MUSIC'S ALL AROUND

SAM.

AND IT'S MORE THAN JUST WHAT'S PLAYIN'

CARLY.

IT'S EVERYTHING THAT STARTS TO SING WHEN WE'RE ALL
IN TUNE

SAM & MELANIE.

I GOT YOU WITH ME

LOLA.

AND AS LONG AS WE ARE STAYIN'

ALL BUT ROBERT.

I AIN'T LETTIN' GO OF YOU ANY DAY SOON

ROBERT.	**ALL BUT ROBERT.**
SOMEWHERE LIVIN' KEEPS ON GOIN'	YOU.

ROBERT.

BUT AIN'T NO HEAVEN LIKE YOUR COMPANY
I AIN'T SCARED TO LEAVE NOW KNOWIN'
I SPENT MY LIFE WITH MY CHOSEN FAMILY

*(Music changes as the dancing slows and
the couples begin to slow dance;* **CARLY** *looks
on...)*

Scene Seven (A): Winter / Transition to Scene Eight

[MUSIC NO. 22 "WINTER"]

(**JOEL** *and* **ELIZABETH** *stand at their microphones; singing the song as though it is the last slow dance of the evening. At the same time, the fall foliage is stripped from the scene as though taking down the Southern Comfort décor for the year.*)

JOEL.

I HOLD ONTO THE DAY
BUT WE'RE LOSING IT ANYWAY

ELIZABETH.

WE GET LESS OF IT NOW THAN I EVER HAVE SEEN

BOTH.

STRETCHING NIGHTS IN BETWEEN US FULL OF WORDS
    WE
WON'T SAY

JOEL.

WON'T EVEN WHISPER

ELIZABETH.

WON'T EVEN WHISPER

(*Lights fade on* **CARLY**.)

BOTH.

THEY TELL ME IT'S WINTER AND THAT'S JUST THE WAY
THEY TELL ME IT HAPPENS NOW AND AGAIN
THEY TELL ME IT'S CRUEL AND IT ENDS SOME DAY
WELL I DON'T KNOW IF I CAN WAIT UNTIL THEN

(**MELANIE** *and* **SAM** *exit.*)

ELIZABETH.

I HOLD ONTO THE DAY
BUT I'M LOSING IT ANYWAY

JOEL.

I BEEN DRAGGING IT RIGHT HERE ALONG SIDE OF ME

BOTH.

WHILE THE SHUDDERING BREEZE WHISPERS WHAT WE
WON'T SAY

WHAT WE WON'T SAY

> (**LOLA** *lets go of* **ROBERT** *and exits so that*
> **ROBERT** *stands alone in a spot of light... The*
> *scene is fully stripped of foliage and color –*
> *bare.*)

LET ME SURRENDER

> (**ROBERT** *surveys his surroundings as he is*
> *illuminated in a spot of light. A separate spot*
> *illuminates* **JACKSON** *in another place.*)

ELIZABETH.

LET ME SURRENDER

JOEL.

LET ME SURRENDER

ELIZABETH.

LET ME SURRENDER

JOEL.

LET ME SURRENDER

ELIZABETH.

LET ME SURRENDER

BOTH.

SURRENDER...

> (*Lights fade on all but* **JACKSON**. *There is a*
> *lingering darkness around him, then a match*
> *pierces the dark and is used to ignite a pipe. A*
> *moment as the pipe glows orange. We cannot*
> *see who is smoking it, just a ghostly shape.*
> **JACKSON** *looks on fondly for a moment...*)

Scene Eight: Robert's House

> *(Lights expand around the glowing pipe to reveal **LOLA** sitting in a chair on Robert's porch. She puffs at the pipe somewhat awkwardly, then promptly begins to cough and hack.)*

JACKSON. You take up smokin' now?

> *(Startled at first that someone is there – doubly startled to see **JACKSON**.)*

LOLA. *(With a cough.)* Jackson!

> *(Then, in reference to the pipe, still clearing her lungs:)*

Oh, no. I just light it some nights, the smell...and just seein' it there – it reminds me o' Robert.

JACKSON. Oh...

> *(A moment.)*

Sorry; didn't think anyone would be here. I was just comin' by to... You know...

LOLA. Not really. No.

> *(...)*

We're havin' a little get-together Sunday to say a proper goodbye. If you want, you can –

JACKSON. Oh, well, I got an appointment on Monday. Not supposed to eat n' drink n' stuff the day before, so –

LOLA. Oh. For your surgery. You're really getting it done.

JACKSON. Really.

> *(A beat.)*

How 'bout you. You doin' anything new?

LOLA. Nothing. No.

JACKSON. Oh. You're livin' here now?

LOLA. Squatting's more like it.

JACKSON. Didn't Robert –

LOLA. Didn't Robert...what? Leave me the house? Is that why you're here, you want me to read you the will?

(*A moment.* **LOLA** *looks a bit guilty for what she's said.*)

He left it to all of us. He wanted us to keep meeting here on Sundays.

JACKSON. And you didn't bother to tell me?

LOLA. There was nothin' to tell. Robert was behind on payments... Bank's foreclosing and it'll be gone soon.

JACKSON. Gone? How did this happen?

LOLA. I don't know, Jackson. It wasn't –

JACKSON. What were y'all doin' here: playin' house?

LOLA. What?

JACKSON. Do you even realize how much this meant to him?

LOLA. Of course I do. Do you even realize how much you meant to him? Because you didn't have any problem takin' that away, did you?

JACKSON. I didn't take anything away.

LOLA. You took his family, Jackson.

JACKSON. His family changed. Chosen Family, right?

LOLA. No. Choosing your family means committing to who they are and what they become.

JACKSON. Someone shoulda told Robert that.

[MUSIC NO. 23 "GIVING UP THE GHOST"]

LOLA. That's enough, Jack.

I CAN'T HELP YOU FIGHT A FIGHT
I DIDN'T EVEN START
I CAN'T FACE YOUR DEMONS
WHILE OUR FAM'LY FALLS APART

I CAN'T TELL YOU ANYTHING
YOU WISH YOU COULD HAVE HEARD
I CAN'T SPEAK FOR SOMEONE WHO
CAN'T SAY ANOTHER WORD

HE IS DONE

WITH THE FIGHT
HE WAS FIGHTING ALL HIS LIFE
GIVING EVERYONE THE MOST
WE WERE LOVED
WE WERE KNOWN
HE'S THE HEART THAT BROUGHT US HOME
UNTIL HE GAVE UP THE GHOST

BUT I KNEW OUR TIME WAS SHORT
BEFORE OUR TIME BEGAN
I WAS RUNNING AFTER HIM
THE SAME TIME THAT YOU RAN

CUZ WE KNOW
HOW TO RUN
FROM THE PLACES WE COME FROM
NEVER HOPING FOR THE MOST
LIKE THE BEST
WE COULD DO
WAS TO SIMPLY MAKE IT THROUGH
UNTIL GIVING UP THE GHOST

SO I COULD STAND HERE FIGHTING YOU
BUT YOU ALREADY KNOW
EVERYTHING YOU LOST BY LETTING EVERYBODY GO
IT'S NOT HARD TO UNDERSTAND
THE INSTINCT JUST TO RUN
BUT MY UNDERSTANDING CAN'T CHANGE WHAT YOU'VE
    DONE
AND COMING HERE WON'T BRING BACK ANYONE

> (**JACKSON** *is overwhelmed and, after a beat,*
> *he exits.* **LOLA** *collects herself in his absence;*
> *moving back to Robert's pipe.*)

I DIDN'T KNOW
WHAT I'D DO
WHEN I HAD TO GIVE UP YOU
IT'S THE DAY I FEARED THE MOST
BUT WHAT YOU
SAW IN ME
SHOWED ME I COULD BE COMPLETE

WITHOUT GIVING UP THE GHOST
I'M NOT GIVING UP THE GHOST
I'M NOT GIVING UP THE GHOST

> (**ROBERT'S PARENTS** *are illuminated behind* **LOLA** *as she still faces downstage...*)

Scene Nine: Robert's Parents' House

(**LOLA** *nervously faces the audience; we understand that she is addressing* **ROBERT'S PARENTS***, illuminated upstage of her, also facing the audience.*)

LOLA. Hello? Mr. and Mrs. Eads?

ROBERT'S FATHER. Who're you?

LOLA. I'm Lola.

ROBERT'S FATHER. Who?

ROBERT'S MOTHER. Wait... Lola? Ain't that... You're Barbara's, uh...

LOLA. Robert. I'm Robert's "...uh."

ROBERT'S FATHER. Okay. Well?

LOLA. I'm here to... Robert passed away.

(*A long silence.*)

ROBERT'S MOTHER. *What?*

LOLA. I'm so sorry.

ROBERT'S MOTHER. When? *How?*

LOLA. He'd been sick for a while. He so wanted to tell you, but...it was too much.

ROBERT'S MOTHER. Too much? To tell us she was... Why? Why did she –

LOLA. He. It was cancer. Ovarian cancer.

ROBERT'S FATHER. Get off our property.

ROBERT'S MOTHER. But –

LOLA. Please. I know that he –

ROBERT'S FATHER. Barb died o' bein' a woman and you got the nerve to come here still callin' her "he"?

LOLA. Yes. I don't know who Barbara was, but Robert... if this world were a different place – a fair place – he would have been king of some country or President of the United States. He was that kind of man.

And that don't come from nowhere. So like it or not, you raised the most amazing person I've ever had the privilege of knowing.

> *(A moment, then the spots dim on* **ROBERT'S PARENTS** *as* **LOLA** *moves downstage...)*

As per his request, we spread his ashes underneath the Christmas tree in his yard.

Scene Ten: The Tree

> (LOLA *finishes moving downstage as lights reveal* MELANIE, SAM, *and* CARLY, *standing in the same positions as in the opening tableau around the small evergreen tree. A few disparate/mismatched ornaments hang on its branches.* MELANIE *hands* LOLA *an ornament, and* LOLA *continues toward the tree, hanging her ornament on one of the branches.*)

LOLA. So now...even though it'll soon be someone else's home...this tree...this will always be Robert's little piece o' Toccoa.

> (JACKSON *enters, unseen by the others, as* LOLA *approaches the tree and hangs an ornament on it.* CARLY *notices him.*)

CARLY. *Jack.*

JACKSON. Hey.

> (*Everyone turns.*)

LOLA. Oh, I thought –

...What about your appointment?

JACKSON. I cancelled it.

> (*Everyone looks to* LOLA – *an absent-minded gesture of "new leadership."*)

LOLA. Well...we already spread his ashes, now we're just... each sayin' somethin'.

JACKSON. Okay. Could I say somethin'?

> (*Silence.*)

...I wanna say it to all o' you really. Just... I'm sorry. I know there's nothing I can say to get back the time we lost...

And I know there's no forgivin' me for not bein' here when Robert...when he...

LOLA. Died. He died, Jackson.

JACKSON. *(A beat to maintain his composure.)* ...I just... I couldn't handle losin' him... Not like that. Felt like losin' everything. The whole war, you know? And the stupidest thing is; I made myself think I was bein' strong in stayin' away. But then; Lola, you reminded me – choosin' your family is a commitment you can't just run away from. So I ain't runnin' away. And it might be too late, I know: but I'm hopin'... I mean, I'd like us to meet here next Sunday too. And the next Sunday. And the next –

LOLA. We can't. Not here.

JACKSON. Like Heck we can't.

CARLY. Jack, It wasn't Robert's to give anymore.

JACKSON. But it can still be ours to take.

SAM. Everything we got together won't even cover a down payment. And any extra any o' us had went to goin' to SoCo this year.

JACKSON. Well I just so happen to have a little bit set aside.

MELANIE. How could you –

LOLA. Your savings.

> *(He nods.)*

But that's...

That's for you, Jack. We can't ask you to –

[MUSIC NO. 24/25 "HOME/SPRING (REPRISE)"]

JACKSON. You ain't askin'. And I ain't givin' you any choice. This is our ground for Christ – for *Pete's* sake...

IT MIGHT NOT BE SO GREAT AND WIDE
IT MIGHT MAKE SOME FOLK STARE
IT MIGHT BE PEELIN' FROM THE SIDES AND NEEDIN'
   SOME REPAIR

IT MIGHT NOT LOOK LIKE MUCH TODAY
WITH ONE SAD LONELY TREE
IT MIGHT BE MILES AND MILES AWAY FROM WHERE FOLK
   SAY IT SHOULD BE, OH

THERE'S SOME BRICKS OUT BY THE FENCE THERE
WHERE THE GRASS IS GROWIN' TALL
A PILE O' GOOD INTENTIONS THAT WAS SUPPOSED TO BE
    A WALL
YEAH IT'S BROKEN DOWN AND BEATEN
IT'S DONE EVERYTHING BUT FALL
AND NO ONE BUT THE FEW OF US KNOW WHAT'S REALLY
    HERE AT ALL

THEY CAN CALL IT UGLY AS SIN
FOR EVERYTHING IT SHOWS
BUT HOME DON'T HIDE BENEATH ITS SKIN, OR
    UNDERNEATH ITS CLOTHES
IT FINDS COMFORT DEEP WITHIN, AND FROM THAT
    GROUND
IT GROWS...

(A moment, then **JACKSON** *turns and looks about to leave. The others all look to* **LOLA***, who steps away from the tree, approaching* **JACKSON***.)*

LOLA. Before Robert passed – he was in and out a lot, sayin' nonsense mostly. But one of the last things he said that made sense was: He told me how proud he is of you.

LIZZIE.
    SOMETHING REAL UNDERNEATH THE COLD

LOLA. Well...his exact words were that you're pig-headed; you're stubborn; you don't give a damn what anyone thinks: And he wouldn't have his son any other way.

DAVID.
    SOMETHING TRUE AND TRYIN' TO TAKE HOLD

LOLA. *(Handing* **JACKSON** *an ornament.)* Happy Sunday, Jack.

ELIZABETH.
    SOMETHING CAN'T WAIT ANYMORE TO START

JACKSON. Happy Sunday, Lola.

JOEL.
    SOMETHING AT THE WALLS INSIDE YOUR HEART

LIZZIE.

SOMETHING SOMEBODY ONCE SAID TO YOU

DAVID.

HAUNTS YOU LIKE A BITTER STING

ELIZABETH.

SOMETHING IN YOU KNOWS IT ISN'T TRUE...

ALL.

LET IT UP AND LET IT SPRING... AHHH
DOWN WITH LIVING YOUR LIFE UNDER THERE
UP WITH SPRING
OH SPRING UP
UP WITH SPRING
OH SPRING UP
UP WITH SPRING
OH SPRING UP
UP WITH SPRING
OH SPRING UP EVERYWHERE

> (**JACKSON** *has hung his ornament on the tree. Lights fade on the group, so that only the tree – sparsely decorated with five ornaments – remains illuminated.*)

EVERYWHERE
EVERYWHERE...

> (*Curtain.*)

9 780573 705458